# The Maid and the Mid

## A Supernatural Sea Story

Jennifer Newbold

The Maid and the Mid

Copyright © 2024 by Jennifer Newbold



Yesterday Press
124 Hillcrest Rd.
Concord, MA 01742

*For Steve, who makes it all possible*

# The Maid and the Mid

## PART I

My daughter and I watch the elaborately decorated funeral car pass from our window fronting on the Strand. The coffin in its richly-embroidered pall looks very small and slightly lost under the high, black-plumed canopy, and the application of a ship's bow and stern to the car strike me as slightly too literal. But there is no doubt it is extraordinary. A state funeral for a commoner.

I sigh. I hope that wherever his soul resides now, it is gratified by this extravagant tribute. If only the government had seen fit to honour him thus when he was alive. Maybe he would not have made quite such a controversial figure of himself, chasing glory… I feel a long-delayed grief grab me by the throat, and I swallow, trying to force it away. I blink away the tears that threaten to smear my spectacles, and steal a look at Catherine.

*She has turned out to be more beautiful than I could have imagined.* Soon to be a mother herself, her golden hair, pulled back from her face and flowing in glorious waves down her back and over her shoulder, reminds me of my own when I met him. It was always my best quality, but in my youth a modest young woman kept her hair pulled up under her cap, and a man did not see it in all its glory until we were wed.

There are tears shining in Catherine's eyes, and I slip my arm around her shoulder and pull her close. 'Do not dare cry, love, or I shall, too,' I admonish her.

'I'm a goose,' she admits, dabbing her cornflower-blue eyes with a dainty, lace-trimmed handkerchief; she has always been more ladylike than I ever was. I shall never know where those eyes came from. My eyes are blue, but with a band of hazel around the pupil, and her father's eyes were grey. 'I didn't even know the man, and here I am, inclined to weep because he's gone. I cry at every little thing lately.'

'I daresay most of those people out there did not know him either,' I say, rather more sadly than I intended, 'and I see many handkerchiefs in fists. Once this child is born, you will no longer feel like crying at the drop of a pin, my darling. You may feel overwhelmed, admittedly, and sometimes exhausted, and occasionally overwrought, but you will not have time to feel sentimental.'

'So you keep telling me.' She looks fondly at me, and her lovely forehead creases. 'Mama, you look positively bereft. I have not seen you look so since Papa died. Has this put you in mind of him?'

'I never forget your father, Kate. But no; I am thinking of Lord Nelson, a long time ago.' Looking at the street, I see the procession of mourners following the funeral car, and the crowds lining the pavements, but in my mind I see a young man, very far from home; as was I, but at least my family was with me. He was, for all intents and purposes, alone.

I spoke quietly, but this statement draws her attention away from the funeral procession like a candle flame will draw a moth. 'What? Did you know him?!'

'I met him. I am not sure how well I can claim to have *known* him…' *Perhaps not as well as I might have liked to, had circumstances been different.*

She sniffles prettily, but her moment of sentiment is past, conquered by curiosity. 'You must tell me about him! Please… was he always such a… *unfathomable* creature?'

'Do you mean, was he always an heroic man with an impulsive streak, constantly seeking approbation? I suppose the foundation of a person's character does not change much over the course of a life, but he was a very young man when I met him. We were both little more than children at the time.'

'That does not exactly answer my question.' *Oh, she can be persistent, my daughter, and whilst she is lovely, she is far from empty-headed.* It appears that I will have to tell this story, whether I can do it with composure, or not. I try to banish the image of that small, lonely coffin, because if I do not, I will certainly break down.

'Come back to the fire, then. It's cold here by the window, and the light will soon be gone. I'll ask Betty to bring us tea. Would you like bread and butter, or cake?'

It was almost thirty years ago when my father took our family to Calcutta. Things had been very bad in Bengal, and he was to advise the new governor general, Mr Hastings. We had lived Calcutta for almost two years when my father was called back to England. Now everything *was going to the Devil'*, to use Papa's words, in the American colonies, and my father was of more value to the King in London than in Calcutta. The colonists do not want to pay their taxes. *Nobody wants to pay taxes; what makes the American colonists think they're exceptional?*

We sailed past Ceylon and around Cape Comorin to Bombay. It seems as though it would be faster to go overland, but the mountains are impenetrable and the interior inhospitable, home to all manner of dangerous creatures. This was only the first leg of our journey home. I remembered the voyage to Calcutta two years before, and how interminable it had been… I had been thirteen when we left England, and I turned fourteen mid-way through the six-month's-long passage. I had not minded it as much as Clarice, my older sister. She was ill every time the sea turned rough.

Reecy was not returning to England with us, though. Six months ago she had married Captain William Clark, a regular army captain—*not* of the East India Company, he was always quick to point out—and was expecting a baby. Captain Clark's proposal had put my parents all afluster. They had envisioned a gentleman husband for Reecy, and while Captain Clark was indeed a gentleman, he was a *military* gentleman. Nevertheless, my sister and her beau won out, and they both seemed blissfully happy. I envied my sister's freedom from our parents, just a little. She described her contract with her husband as a 'partnership', as opposed to a patriarchy. I hoped for the same one day.

We had to cool our heels for a while in Bombay, until a ship arrived to take us for the *long haul*. Bombay was a Company town, a fortified island. The Royal Navy tended to base their ships here in the wintertime, but although it was winter in England, it was summertime in Bombay. By the time we reached home, it would be summertime in London.

Bombay was very clean and well-ordered, but quite martial. I did not see as many native faces as in Calcutta, apart from the sepoys, the native soldiers. And there were few people with which to socialise, apart from the Company officers. There were far fewer women here than in Calcutta, and none my own age; I was quickly bored to tears.

I had always been of the opinion that a ship was a ship, but I was underwhelmed by HMS *Dolphin*. A 24-gun full-rigged ship, she was the smallest class of frigate, and had she been a person, I would have said she looked ailing. Tobias, my older brother, told me that was a good thing; pirates would leave her alone, because she was no prize.

My brother could always be counted on to say something unsettling.

It was on account of Tobias that I made Horace's acquaintance at all, so I suppose I shouldn't be sardonic, but Tobias and I always did enjoy baiting one another a little. When we were young, Clarice was always 'Reecy', and I was 'Annie', but Tobias was always Tobias, *never* 'Toby'. He would not have it, and I was sometimes frustrated by his stubborn rejection of this harmless familiarity.

On our first night at sea, on deck by the bow, Tobias told me the legend of the *Flying Dutchman*. I suppose he'd thought me too young when we journeyed to Calcutta, and had been holding it gleefully in reserve for our voyage home. Either that, or he'd learnt it since.

'She's a phantom Dutch East Indiaman, lost off the Cape of Good Hope almost twenty years ago, with all hands, in a raging sea. She's manned by spirits, and they say that if you see her, it foretells your doom,' he said in a confidential voice, as we looked out over a calm sea, where mist was beginning to gather.

I shivered deliciously. Without much effort I could imagine her materializing out of the mist, her sails in rags.

'They say that her masts and yards glow with a ghostly light, and her crew is damned to sail the seas forever,' Tobias continued spookily. 'If you see her in a gale, you'll go to the bottom with her. We shall sail right past the position where she went down, you know…'

'Alright, that's quite enough,' I told him, swatting his shoulder.

He gazed around. 'Imagine how many people have died on this ship,' he whispered dramatically.

'People die everywhere, Tobias. If we all became spirits the entire world would be teeming with ghosts.'

'But if *nobody* ever became a ghost we wouldn't have any stories about them, would we?'

That was not meant to be a question, and he made sure to be gone before I came up with a rejoinder. Tobias liked to have the last word.

It was late, and Mama was asleep when I got up to use the necessary. There was a chamber pot provided in the cabin from which we had displaced the first lieutenant, but

I didn't like to wake Mama, I told myself. Truthfully, that was something of a disingenuous excuse. I have always been fastidious about using the pot, and would not do it unless there was no alternative, or the weather so foul it would be foolish to go out to the privy. I do not like the idea of someone having to empty my body waste. Reecy used to tell me that we all have our lot in life, and someone's lot is to clean the chamber pot, but she couldn't convince me. Until we lived in Bengal, that is, and we were warned always to check the privy for dangerous creatures before we went in, especially at night. I learnt to use the chamber pot then, but I always felt exposed and uncomfortable.

The place where the ordinary sailors do their business is on the beak head, but there's an enclosed seat-of-ease just aft of the bulkhead, for the midshipmen and junior officers. We've been afforded the privilege of using that.

I tapped hesitantly at the door. What if there was a person inside? It was very dark on this deck at night, and to come across anyone in this gloom would be unsettling. Tobias' story about the phantom ship sailed suddenly into my head, most unwelcome.

Hearing nothing, I pushed open the door and quickly did what I needed to do. I did not want to be discovered here any more than I wanted to discover someone else. It was as dark as a root cellar at midnight in there, too.

On our outward passage, Tobias, true to his usual form, had pointed out the pissdale, where the sailors make their water. 'Why do they not just do it over the side…?' I had whispered.

'Probably because it would be an affront to the King's honour to go into battle in a ship with piss-streaks down her sides,' Tobias murmured conspiratorially in my ear, and I had snickered silently into my mitt. I admit, rather shamefacedly now, to having stationed myself inconspicuously near the pissdale, trying to catch a glimpse of a man's thing, but I never did. I probably was not inconspicuous at all.

I am sure it was only my subconscious mind that made me think then of Mr Tremaine, the handsome dark-haired midshipman with the flashing brown eyes. I had made his acquaintance that afternoon. Thomas, his first name was, but I had heard one of his fellow midshipmen call him 'Tommy', and it lodged in my memory. Thus it was that I was thinking of Tommy as I exited the necessary. I suppose it would have been worse had I been thinking about the *Dutchman*.

I made sure the latch was caught, so the door wouldn't swing open and bang as the ship rolled. Her movement was more pronounced than it had been when we retired, and the single night-lanthorn swung from its beam, conjuring shadows that loomed and retreated from the lanthorn's light. I had put one careful foot forward when I heard the sound.

It was a low moan, barely audible, but it made my hair stand on end. I froze, completely unable to move my other foot.

It came again, a drawn-out '*ohhhhh…*' There might have been the breath of a word in the groan at the end, but I didn't stay to listen. I nearly lost my slipper as I bolted, scampering down the deck as fast as I could go without careening into anything in the gloom.

Lying in our berth next to my mother, once my heart stopped pounding and my breathing had returned to normal, I considered the sound. It had almost sounded like a plea. The spirit of some poor tar pleading with the gods, or demons, for his life? It was fine to entertain scary stories here, safely stowed away in our tiny cabin, but unless I wanted to use the chamber pot at night for the next six months, I had better get to the bottom of that noise pretty quickly.

The day dawned overcast and blustery. It was a bit of a challenge to eat, and Tobias turned green and left the table in a hurry. Like Reecy, he didn't have the best sea legs. He was probably getting wet, too.

I found Tobias' overcoat in his cabin and donned my cloak to go above. It wasn't hard to find my brother, who was clinging to the leeward rail in the waist, looking miserable. I put his coat around his shoulders and rubbed his back for a minute while he retched. 'Poor you,' I crooned.

'Thank you for bringing my coat, Annie,' he croaked. 'You're an angel. Now go away. I don't need you to watch me spew.'

I gave his shoulder a practical pat. On my way back down the companion ladder I met my father, who gave me a discerning look. 'Sent you away?' he guessed.

'Oh, yes; but I imagine he'd feel better for having you keep him company until he… feels better,' I told him.

He kissed my forehead. 'Good girl,' he murmured before making his way up.

I was putting my cloak away when I heard the bosun's whistle. It meant the ship was going to change course, and all the hands were needed on the lines. I got pretty good at understanding the bosun's calls on the trip to Calcutta, but I've forgotten most of it now.

This would be an ideal time to investigate the forward part of the deck where I'd heard those sounds last night. Telling myself it was likely the wind in the hawse hole, or something like that, I walked casually towards the foremost bulkhead, looking (I hoped) nonchalant.

My father had always told us to face down our fears, whether it was snakes in the cistern, or the old native woman who begged in the marketplace, who spit at us and cursed in Bengali. Mama told us we should be compassionate, because she lost all her family in the famine. But we were not to engage with her: she would not have appreciated *British* charity.

This particular fear, I told myself, was undoubtedly my imagination.

With all the gunports closed against the rising sea, it was almost as dark as it had been last night, and the lanthorn still rocked with the motion of the ship, drawing the shadows out, then chasing them back again. I looked into the dark recesses between each gun, seeing nothing much, but certainly nothing unusual. *Wind in the hawse hole. Had to have been.*

I was about to go find something else to do when I heard it. That same low moan, or groan, or whatever it was.

I crept forward on my toes as the sound faded out. I paused, then inched closer to the spot where I perceived the sound had come from.

The bulkhead here was of stretched canvas, like the wall of a tent. I heard something shift on the other side of it, followed by a rather piteous, very human, whimper.

'Who's there?' I demanded. The noise stopped dead, as if someone had muffled a bell with their hand. 'Here, was that you, last night?' I continued. 'Are you trying to scare me? If you are, it's an ungentlemanly trick.'

'Who are you…?' asked a thin voice. This wasn't a phantom. It sounded like a boy.

'I'm a passenger. Why are you making that noise, if not to scare decent folk?'

'I'm *ill*,' said the voice indignantly. 'And they've left me alone here.'

'Who has left you alone?'

'The mate. There's no one here but me.'

'Do you mean that they've shut you up there and no one has come to tend to you since we sailed?' I asked, astonished.

'No; the mate comes to check on me, and they bring me meals, if I can eat them. But most of the time they leave me to lie here like deadwood.'

'Look, it's very inconvenient to talk thought this sheet of canvas. Can I come in there?'

'If you like,' said the voice.

I waited. 'How would I do that?' I asked finally.

'Oh… on the opposite side from the lanthorn. The bulkhead doesn't go all the way to the wall.'

If I'd only come around the other side of the foremost gun, I'd have seen that. So much for my method of investigation.

The possessor of the voice did indeed look ill. He might have been my age, but he was so thin and pale that he looked like a boy.

He was lying curled on his side in a canvas cot, a lanthorn suspended nearby so he could be examined easily, I guessed. Even in the light, I got the impression that there was little more to him than pale, shaggy hair and huge, soft eyes. His cheekbones stood out sharply, and his mouth was drawn.

'I'm Anne,' I said. 'How do you do?'

He snorted. 'Not very well, thank you.'

'Do you need anything? Is there something I could bring you?'

He sighed. 'No. I *can* get up, if I need to. But my limbs are so weak I can hardly use them. My arm gets tired when I'm doing nothing more than drinking soup. I can get from here to the seat-of-ease and back again, but barely.' He had the grace to blush, and for a moment I felt for him.

'I am actually quite improved—for a while I could not do anything for myself. They had to take care of me like an infant.' He glanced up at me with those doe-like eyes… if deer had blue eyes. 'I must have committed some dreadful sin of pride at some point. I have been thoroughly humbled,' he muttered.

He was huddled beneath a blanket, even though it was very warm; and a fresh breeze blew through the space, which made it rather pleasant. But he shivered as I watched.

'You cannot possibly be cold,' I commented. 'Is it the draught?'

'Ague,' he said shortly. 'The paroxysms were lessening, but they've come back. I suppose that's why they've said I must go home. They say I won't get better here. I'm not the only one,' he added defensively. 'I'm just worse than the others right now.'

I looked around the space. 'Would you like me to get you another blanket…? If you can tell me where to find one.'

'Chest there. On your right. Yes, that one.'

I opened the chest and retrieved a blanket, which I unfolded and laid over his cot. He pulled it around himself and shivered for a few moments more, then gradually his shivering ceased. 'It will come back again, but I am alright for the moment,' he said, sounding dreadfully tired.

'Is this the fever that all the English people in Calcutta dreaded? Mama insisted that we all drink some bitter tincture made from bark every day to keep it off.'

'Peruvian bark. Yes.'

'I think she called it Jesuit's.'

'Same thing, I think.' He winced. 'Sometimes it makes me sick to my stomach. Other times, I think it's the fever that does it.'

'Is that why you are so dreadfully thin?' I asked, with concern.

'I suppose so.'

'I'm sorry I accused you of trying to scare me, if you really only had the stomach-ache. Let's start again, and I'll be civilised to you this time. My name is Anne Middleton. I'm pleased to make your acquaintance.'

'Horatio Nelson,' he said. 'Likewise.'

'Would you like me to go away and let you rest, Horatio Nelson?'

'No,' he said, as emphatically as I'd heard him say anything yet. 'Please, stay and talk to me. Take my mind away from how miserable I feel.'

'Very well. I shall be happy to talk to you. I have no one else to talk to, except my family. Everyone else aboard seems to have a job to do.'

'I have duties, too, once I'm well enough.'

'Have you? What do you do?'

'I am a midshipman. Hand me that book, there.'

I picked it up from the table and gave it to him. 'I am studying for the lieutenant's exam,' he said, caressing the cover. His wrist bones didn't even fill the wrist band of his shirt.

'You are starting early, aren't you?'

'Rather. I'll be eighteen in September, and technically one cannot be made lieutenant until twenty.'

I tried not to let my surprise show. 'You are seventeen?'

'I know,' he said ruefully. 'People rarely believe me when I tell them my age.'

'It's nothing to be ashamed of.'

'I think I have to work twice as hard as other people, because I look like a child, so they think me incapable.'

'I do not know you at all, but I am sure you are not incapable. Ordinarily,' I added, and then felt bad for doing so, but he didn't take offense.

'What were you doing in the East Indies, Miss Middleton?'

'My father was working with the governor in Bengal. It was quite exotic, living in Calcutta, at first. But I am glad to go home. I am so tired of dampness! Either it is hot and damp, or cool and damp, but it is *never* cool and dry. And I am afraid of snakes.'

'I come from Norfolk, where it is marshy, and I have lived upon ships for the last five years; I suppose I am accustomed to damp. But are there many snakes in Calcutta?'

'There are four very dangerous snakes in Calcutta, and I cannot tell one snake from another. Therefore, I am afraid of all of them.' Just talking about them made me shudder.

'You should learn which ones are dangerous,' he suggested. 'Then you wouldn't need to be afraid of most of them.'

'That's easy for you to say. There are no snakes on a ship.'

'They could come in with the provisions,' he said, and if he'd been Tobias I might have swatted him. He must have seen the expression on my face, because he added quickly, 'If they did, they'd be down in the hold, though, so as long as you never go down there, you will be fine.'

'I have no desire to go down in the hold,' I assured him. 'And it was far easier and less frightening simply to avoid every snake, and never go out into the gardens at night, for the really dangerous ones are nocturnal. The gardener pointed out a krait to me once, when we were newly arrived in Calcutta. I thought it looked rather friendly, with little black button eyes, but he told me that it was an extremely irritable snake whose bite could kill me in four hours, and although I would not feel his bite, I would quickly suffocate to death.'

My companion went paler than he had been before, which I would not have thought possible. I said quickly, 'I'm sorry, I did not mean to upset you. Do forget about the krait. Unless you return to India, you will probably never see one.'

He shook his head, curling up in the middle in the manner of a wood louse. 'It's… not the snake,' he groaned.

'Oh dear. It's your stomach, isn't it? Do you feel like you might vomit? Is there a basin somewhere…?'

'It… will pass… in a minute. I shan't be sick… I think.'

I swiftly searched the area with my eyes anyway, and spied the basin beneath his cot. 'Just to be on the safe side,' I said, picking it up.

He closed his eyes and moaned softly, and now it didn't sound eerie at all. It sounded only like a young man in pain. Moved by his suffering, I switched the basin to my left hand, rubbing his back gently with my right as I'd done for Tobias earlier.

I felt his rigid muscles gradually begin to relax, and he took a shuddering breath. I stepped away as his body unclenched and he collapsed flat against his pillow. He did not open his eyes or acknowledge me.

'I hope I have not been too familiar,' I said hesitantly. 'Perhaps it was not the appropriate thing to do.'

He looked at me then, his face almost as pale as the linen slip on his pillow. 'It was kind of you,' he murmured.

'If completely ineffective,' I finished. 'I am sorry. I was rubbing my brother's back when he was being seasick this morning. I don't know why I thought it might help you.'

'I appreciated it,' he said softly. 'It… gave me something to think about besides the sickness.' He let his eyes fall shut again. 'My feet are so cold,' he muttered, more to himself than to me.

I looked around again, seeing nothing that might help ease cold feet. 'Since I've already been too familiar with you once, would you… would you like me to hold them? Perhaps that would help warm them up.'

His reaction belied his child-like appearance. 'What would my comrades think of me if I declined to let a pretty maid hold my feet?' he said wryly. 'If you are willing to do that, I would be honoured, Miss Middleton.'

I moved aside his blankets and grasped one of his bare feet. It *was* cold. I was surprised. 'Have you woollen stockings, Mr Nelson?'

'You must call me Horace, since you are now intimately acquainted with my right foot. Yes, there are some woollen stockings in my chest, beneath my cot.'

'You do not mind if I open it?'

'I am in too humble a position already, to be embarrassed by the state of my sea chest. Open it. If it is not too much of a jumble, the stockings should be on the left, in the back.'

I unbuckled the straps and lifted the lid of the chest. It was a bit of a welter inside, but the stockings were where he'd said they would be, and it was no worse than the state of Tobias' trunk. Rather better, actually. I closed it and did up the straps again.

'Tell me about your brother,' he said faintly, as I clasped his foot in my hands again.

'Tobias? Tobias is nineteen, and my father has been training him in diplomacy. He's fairly good at it, except with me. We have no diplomacy with each other. We rather enjoy a bit of good-natured teasing; he would not be my brother if he suddenly stopped teasing me. I hope he shall still tease me when we're old, about who has the more accomplished grandchildren, or whatever. I do not tease him about being seasick, though. It must be most unpleasant.'

He nodded in acknowledgement. 'You have never been seasick, then?'

I shook my head.

'Have you other siblings?' He seemed eager for any kind of conversation at all.

'We have an older sister, Clarise. She is twenty-one, and married to a soldier in Calcutta. She is going to have a baby about the time that we reach England, and Mama was so torn between going home and staying with Clarise that she did not know what to do. Reecy finally told her to go. She loves our mother and father devotedly, but I think she loves her new freedom with her husband more.' I slipped one of the stockings over his toes. His foot was long and narrow, and I thought I could see every bone and tendon. *No wonder they are cold, there is barely any flesh on them.*

He reached down and pulled the stocking up his calf while I took his other foot in my hands. I could see the knee band of his breeches, and I discreetly looked away, but not before I noticed that his leg was so wasted, he could probably stick his whole hand between his calf and the knee band, with it buttoned. I pressed my thumb into his arch, and he responded with a quiet, approving hum. 'That feels nice.'

'If I may call you Horace, then you must call me Anne.' I held the foot for a while, pressing my thumb gently into the arch and moving it in little circles. He did not ask me any more questions, lying back against his pillow with his eyes closed. I used the opportunity to observe him.

I thought he must be of average height, and had probably been nicely proportioned before he became ill, but now he was so terribly thin. His hair seemed to grow in floppy, untameable shocks, like a friendly spaniel, but it too looked pale, drained of colour. He wore it in a queue down his back that reached between his shoulder blades, I had discovered when rubbing his back. Those shoulder blades stuck out like wings beneath his shirt.

His face, when relaxed, was pleasant, albeit thin and drawn. He had a prominent nose with a classic ridge, like the drawings of the busts of the Roman generals I had seen in books. His eyelashes brushed his cheek gracefully. His lower lip was soft and full, but slightly chapped. I wanted to rub sweet almond oil into it, then was shocked at myself for thinking of it.

'Tell me about your own family,' I said, drawing the other stocking over his now warm foot. 'Horace…?'

He sighed but did not reply, and I realised that he was asleep. I pulled the stocking up over his ankle and covered his foot again with the blankets, then I took the lieutenant's exam book from his cot and set it on the table. The light from the lanthorn did not seem to disturb him, so I left it alone. Then I walked softly from the sick berth, mentally wishing him well.

I had not intended to go back to the sick berth to visit the pale, emaciated midshipman, but I lay awake that night, thinking about him. I did not know what had possessed me to touch him like that, a boy I had never met before; if my father knew, he would probably lock me in this cabin just for being alone with him.

*I pity him*, I decided. He seemed so desperate for human companionship, unlike the famine widow, who in her misery wanted to thrust everyone away.

In the morning, after breakfast, I drew my father aside.

'Papa, I met a boy yesterday…' (*Oh, that was quite the wrong way to begin!*) 'He's one of the midshipmen.' (*He's training to be an officer. That's rather better.*) 'But he's in the sick berth, because he's quite ill with fever, the one that Mama always makes us take that awful tincture for.'

My father's brow creased, and I said hurriedly, 'He's all alone there, and dreadfully lonely. I spoke to him through the canvas bulkhead,' *(and I did, too, initially)* 'but I wanted your permission to go and see him today. It's so very well ventilated; I do not think we need worry about contagion.' I judged my father's expression, then added piously, 'Mama tells us we must be compassionate to other people's misfortunes. I think this boy could do with a bit of compassion. Will you come with me, Papa?'

He gave me that look that said he knew that I was attempting to get away with something, but it was an admirable effort. 'Very well, Anne. I will come with you and judge the situation. I will withhold or grant my permission then.'

'Thank you, Papa,' I said soberly, but inside my heart was jubilant.

Papa walked with me to the sick berth, and I stood next to the canvas and called, 'Mr Nelson? It is Anne Middleton. Are you… do you feel up to company?'

There was a pause, and I began to wonder if he was asleep, or not there, but then I heard him say, 'I would welcome company, Miss Middleton, as long as the company does not mind my infirmity. I cannot be a good host today, I am afraid.'

'Then we must be good guests,' I replied, moving to the doorway. 'I have brought my father with me. Papa, this is Mr Horace Nelson. Mr Nelson, this is my father, Mr Edgar Middleton.' I tried signalling with my eyes, to tell him he must not say anything about the day before, but I did not know if Horace could read my optical semaphore.

He was lying in his cot, again quite solitary, and today he looked as limp as a silk handkerchief. The blankets were pushed away, and the woollen stockings I'd put on his feet yesterday were rolled up at the end of the cot. A faint sheen of perspiration covered his brow, and a sheet the lower half of his body; his linen shirt looked almost empty on his narrow breast.

'I am honoured to make your acquaintance, sir. Please forgive my indisposition,' he said. 'This is my fever day. Tomorrow I will be stronger.'

'Your servant, sir,' my father replied. 'May we sit?'

'Please. Do not stand upon ceremony on my behalf,' the patient said faintly.

My father took a chair from the table, and I found a three-legged stool and carried it over. There was a bowl of thin gruel and a mug of some kind of acidulated whey sitting on the table, looking unappealing.

'Is this what they feed you?' I asked disapprovingly.

'It is all I can stomach, if I can stomach anything at all on a fever day. I will make up for it tomorrow.' He struggled to raise himself higher on the pillow.

'Let me help you, sir,' Papa offered, arranging the pillow so it supported his head and bony shoulders. 'My daughter tells me you are a midshipman, Mr Nelson. How long have you served His Majesty?'

'I first took ship at Chatham, five years ago.' He must have been accustomed to he surprised expression on my father's face, because he added, 'I am older than I look.'

'Still, you must have been very young…?'

'I was twelve,' Horace said. 'I have had a good run, even was it to end here.'

'Surely not!' I blurted. He looked at me, and a faint smile flickered across his lips.

'Some days I believe it will not,' he assured me. 'On others, I am not as confident. At least I have the use of my limbs, now.'

His eyes appeared even larger today, in that thin face, and they burned with fever light. His bottom lip looked more chapped than it had the day before, and again I felt sorry for him. 'Is there no one looking after you?'

'The loblolly boy was here shortly before you came, trying to get me to eat, but I have no appetite this morning.'

'You must at least drink something,' my father observed. 'Let me get that mug for you. You cannot sweat out the bad humours if you do not drink enough.' Papa held the mug of whey for him to sip. Horace guided it with his own thin hand, and his finger joints looked bony and frail next to Papa's strong hand. I frowned without quite meaning to.

He must have noticed, because he said to me, 'You look displeased,' as my father returned the mug to the table.

'Why, no; it is only… well, you shouldn't be alone here! There ought to be someone to nurse you. If you wanted that mug, or to… to go… somewhere, would you even be able to get out of that cot?'

'Yes. At least, I think so. I might not be able to get back into it, though.'

'What would you do, if you could not?!'

'I would sit on the floor until someone came to help me. The mate, or the loblolly boy, will look in on me regularly on my fever day, but I do not expect him to sit here constantly at my beck and call. It would quickly become tiresome.' His voice trailed off, as though speaking wore him out. Perhaps it did.

'Your lip looks sore,' I said quietly. 'Is there anything here to put on it?'

'I do not know. No one has ever offered.'

'I have a pot of sweet almond oil and beeswax. I will bring it when I see you next.'

'You are very kind.'

'We are tiring you,' my father observed. 'We will depart and let you rest.'

His eyes, which had been drooping, flew open. 'I am sorry I am not better company today. I hope you will come again, when I might be a better host,' he pleaded.

'I shall, if Papa will allow it,' I asserted.

'We will make sure you do not lack for companionship,' Papa affirmed. 'There are four of us aboard, with nothing much to do for the next six months.'

'I hope your brother is recovered from his seasickness…?' he enquired politely, but I could see he was having to make an effort.

'I'm sure he will be fully himself again in no time at all,' I said. 'Perhaps I might bring him with me tomorrow?'

'I'd like that.'

'You say that now,' I said lightly, and my father frowned, but not reprovingly. Papa knew how it was with me and Tobias, because we had always been this way.

Horace responded with a weak laugh. 'I am sure I will like him,' he murmured.

'Goodbye, then. I hope you are better tomorrow.'

'I shall be, undoubtedly.'

As Papa and I walked together aft, the surgeon's mate passed us, heading for the sick berth, which made me feel less troubled. 'What did you think of him, Papa?'

My father was silent for a moment, then he said gently, 'I hope he makes it home.'

I blinked, and the uneasy feeling descended again.


My apprehension was slightly relieved when I brought Tobias with me to the sick berth the following afternoon. Horace was sitting at the table with his book in hand, making notes, a half-eaten meal pushed aside. He was still pale, but his patterned Indian-cotton dressing gown helped disguise how terribly thin he was.

'Horace, this is my brother, Tobias.'

Horace put down his pen and grasped Tobias' extended hand. 'Don't take offense, but you look the way I've felt for the past two days,' Tobias told him.

'And this is one of my good days,' he said wryly. 'No offense taken. I know I'm not much to look at these days.'

'Were you before?'

Tobias wan't being unkind, and Horace laughed, but I thought it a little unfair. He isn't as handsome as Thomas Tremaine, but he's nice-looking enough. Then I realised that I hadn't thought of Tommy Tremaine in two days.

'So. You are studying to take the lieutenant's exam, Anne said?'

'As soon as they'll allow it.' His eyes shone, and today it wasn't with fever.

Tobias bestowed a critical eye upon him. 'Are you sure you're not delirious? I've just spent two days casting up my accounts over the leeward bulwark, and I daresay it won't be the last time I do, on this trip. Yet you want to make a career of it?'

'Well, not of being seasick, no. The Royal Navy is admittedly not for everyone.'

'You say that as though it's a badge of honour.'

'I believe it is,' he said, with the quiet power of conviction.

'Perhaps I should like to be a sailor,' I said jauntily. 'I do not suffer seasickness.'

'Even were you to run into the *Flying Dutchman?*' Tobias challenged.

'Oh, pooh, Tobias. You and your *Dutchman.* He was trying to frighten me with the *Flying Dutchman* the other night,' I explained.

'You'll have to be a bit more credulous if you're to be a sailor,' Horace said with a smile. 'We're a terribly superstitious lot.'

'Oh? Do tell!'

'Hmm. Well, first you have to learn your Greek sea gods. There are dozens of them. Don't quiz me… I can't remember them all, or what they're all supposed to have done. Poseidon, or Neptune: he's the important one.'

Tobias took up Horace's pen and a sheet of paper. 'Greek sea-gods,' he said as he wrote. 'Check.'

'Never whistle for a wind, and never set sail on a Friday.'

'Check.'

Horace gave me another slight smile. 'You'd have to find yourself a pair of breeches, because women on board are bad luck.'

Tobias blurted a laugh and elbowed me. 'I'll lend you a pair of mine.'

'The blue camlet ones,' I rejoined.

'What? No! Those are my favourites.'

'What else, Horace?' I asked, silencing Tobias.

'A cat aboard is good luck, but if you shoot an albatross, something terrible will happen...'

Tobias scribbled.

'In addition to the *Flying Dutchman*, beware the Kraken, and the Sirens. Either of them will drag you down to Davy Jones's Locker.' He coughed and reached for a pitcher of something at the end of the table, splashing a bit of it into his mug. 'Small beer,' he explained. 'It's not very good, but it's better than it will be six months from now, if you want some.'

Tobias accepted, but I declined, never having much liked small beer. Horace rose carefully and retrieved a second mug, and although his movements were not brisk, he did not seem so terribly weak as he had done the day before.

'In the Mediterranean Sea, in the Strait of Messina, lie Scylla and Charybdis,' he continued, returning with the mug. 'If you sail too close to Scylla, the nymph-turned-monster that lives beneath the mountain, she will lure you onto the rocks and break your ship to bits, then she'll drag you down to the depths of the sea. If you sail too wide, you will be caught by the sea monster Charybdis, whose powerful whirlpool will send your entire ship to the bottom.' He poured small beer into the mug and pushed it across the table to Tobias, whose pen was flying. 'You can find them mentioned in the *Odyssey* and the *Aeneid.*

'St Elmo's fire…' he took a swallow from his mug. 'St Elmo's fire can be interpreted either as good luck or warn of an approaching storm. But storm petrels always presage a storm. Birds are said to be the souls of drowned sailors, warning the ship of danger.'

'There, Anne; there are your ghosts.' Tobias put down the pen and took a gulp of small beer.

'They're birds, Tobias. And they're being helpful, not threatening.'

'That depends on how you interpret them,' Horace said. 'If your ship does not weather the storm, they were not a good omen. Then, there are other phantom ships, probably many of them, I imagine. Two I can think of are the *Octavius*, and *Lady Lovibond,* which is supposed to reappear fifty years after her demise, although I don't think anyone can say where. But she's a ghost ship, so I suppose she could appear anywhere she wants.'

'What about sailors or marines killed in battle? What happens to their souls?' Tobias demanded.

Horace shook his head and cleared his throat. He was beginning to sound slightly hoarse. 'I don't know of any general superstitions about battle deaths. Everyone who dies in battle probably rises in glory, I suppose.'

'Do individual ships have their own ghosts?' I asked.

He frowned. 'I've never served on one that did,' he said slowly. 'We might be superstitious, but I don't think any sailor would tell a ghost story about the place where he had to live for months at a time, out in the middle of the ocean. Not unless he believed it to be true, and I think he'd have to be more than unsettled. I think he would have to be scared witless. Otherwise, it would be malicious mischief, and the ship's officers would have to put a stop to it before it got out of hand.'

'Is there any superstition or legend about that mysterious light, that shimmers in the ship's wake?'

'Some say that's Poseidon, or his naiads, making that glow. Others call it 'the burning of the sea', but it doesn't make enough light to read the binnacle.' He coughed again.

'Look, we're awful guests. We're wearing your voice out,' Tobias observed. 'We should go, let you get on with your studying.'

'No, truly, I'm delighted you're here. It's only that I have not talked this much in months.'

Tobias folded his page of notes and handed it to me. 'Anne has studying to do, too,' he said pointedly. 'I intend to quiz her about everything that's on this sheet.'

'We shall come back and see you again, but you must promise to tell us if you don't feel well enough. You must not think about being polite for our sakes.'

'I'm exceedingly glad you came,' he said earnestly. 'The next time you come, *I* shall ask the questions.'

The next day, however, when I arrived with Mama, he was asleep, and I wrote a consoling note and left it on the table. I had forgotten to bring the pot of almond oil the day before, and I left it on top of my note.

'I hope you and Tobias were not too much for the poor lad yesterday,' she chided me gently, as we walked together on the deck. The sun had returned, and it was already becoming very warm. It would be beastly hot later on.

'I confess I'm a little afraid of that,' I returned, 'but he seemed so much better yesterday, and he was so pleased to have our company.'

'It is a characteristic of his illness, dear, that he has a day or two to recover, but then the paroxysm begins again. If the intermittent fever is tertian, typically the sufferer only gets one day of respite.'

'Poor Horace. He seems so eager for companionship, but the last thing I wish to do is exhaust him. Perhaps I might read to him, do you think? He won't have to wear himself out being engaging, but he'll still have company.'

She frowned gently. 'I shall ask your father,' she said eventually. 'You will have to submit to his decision.'

The question took the form of a family court, with me as the plaintiff. Or perhaps I was arguing Horace's case, and he was the defendant… although he hadn't done anything of which to stand accused, except being male, so that hardly seemed fair.

'He appears to be an honourable young gentleman, but I am unconvinced of the propriety of letting you read to him unchaperoned,' my father said.

'Papa, I am perfectly convinced that he would not do anything blackguardly. And if he tried, first of all, the bulkhead is made of canvas, and you know I can make an ungodly amount of noise if I care to. Secondly, I can certainly outrun him. And thirdly, I do not believe he would do any such thing.'

'You already said that,' Tobias pointed out. 'So that's only two points.' I rolled my eyes at him.

'What would you do if he surprised you, Anne?' Mama asked gravely.

'Well, I… first, I would scream blood— I would scream murder, and brain him with the book, I suppose. And then I'd run like… the wind.' I couldn't imagine braining poor Horace with a book, even if he leered at me like a cad. Which I seriously could not picture at all, but I kept both these thoughts to myself.

'If you want my opinion,' Tobias offered, 'I don't even think the fellow's capable. Not currently.'

'Tobias!' exclaimed our mother.

'I meant strong enough to physically compromise Anne, Mother, not the other thing,' he said hastily. We all knew that he'd meant the other thing.

My father looked at each of us in turn, expressionlessly. He was very good at making his face, and his thoughts, unreadable. Finally, he spoke.

'I have met the young man, and spoken with him, and I believe both my children in this regard, although I deplore the manner in which they have presented their arguments. Anne, you may propose to Midshipman Nelson that you will read to him, if he wishes it. And Tobias, you will safeguard your sister's reputation. You need not be physically present in the sick berth, but I expect you to be close by, very visibly within summoning distance.'

I controlled my satisfaction at this verdict, and said quietly, 'Thank you, Papa,' but inside I felt as though I had won a major victory. Our father was demonstrating his trust in me. And indirectly, in Horace.

'What am I to do, sit outside astride a gun whilst you are with him?' Tobias murmured to me as we adjourned. I smacked him. Rather hard.

'He is not my beau, and don't make filthy jokes,' I said under my breath. 'I should be more wary of *you* corrupting me, than Horace.'

'Sorry,' he said, not altogether contritely. But I knew that despite his flippancy, I could always count on Tobias.

Tobias and I again presented ourselves in the sick berth at mid-morning the following day. Horace didn't look quite as enervated as he had on his last fever day, but he didn't look particularly perky, either.

'Thank you for your note,' he said politely. 'I was disappointed that I missed your visit. I hope I shall meet your mother on another day.'

'You've got six months of Sundays and more,' Tobias said, 'before we set foot in Old England again. Don't worry, you will meet her.'

He really did look disappointed. 'We were afraid perhaps our visit the day before had been too much for you. We might have come back later, but we thought perhaps you needed the rest,' I explained.

'I did sleep rather more than usual,' he admitted quietly, 'but I think it was because I did not have the dreadful stomach pains yesterday, the way I often do. Your visits do me good, I believe.'

'Anne has a proposition—don't look at me like that, Anne—Anne would like to suggest that she would be pleased to read to you, so that if you don't feel like talking, you can just listen. I'm to remain within shouting distance, to ensure that everyone knows that both your virtues remain intact.'

Horace actually blushed, or perhaps it was just a fever flush, but I glared at Tobias. 'You could have put that a bit more diplomatically, Mr Junior Minister.'

'My dear sister, you read beautifully, with exquisite expression, but I have listened to you read aloud for nigh unto twelve years now. I shall sit nearby with my sketch book and act the discreet chaperone. But I know I can depend upon you both to be the essence of propriety. I shall be only the certain sure witness and effectual sign of grace.'

Horace blinked, and I thought he must recognise this mild blasphemy on the Articles of Religion. 'You are tiresome, Tobias,' I said, blushing.

'It is an older brother's duty to be tiresome,' he said with a grin, and walked away.

'I am sorry,' I said to Horace.

'Do not be sorry. I have a tiresome older brother, myself. I love him anyway.'

'That sums it up nicely,' I told him. 'So, what do you think? Would you like me to read to you? To be completely honest, you don't look terribly well...' I realised that this was perhaps I bit too candid. '...although you do look better than you did on your last fever day. But I will go away if you prefer.'

'No, I do not prefer,' he retorted. 'The only person I saw yesterday, apart from the surgeon, the mate, and the loblolly boy, was one of the other midshipmen, who told me how much they were looking forward to having me to share the watches. I appreciate their spirit of camaraderie, as we've never served together before and they certainly have no obligation to me. I didn't have the energy to tell him I'll likely not be standing watches anytime soon.' He rubbed his eyes with a hand that trembled slightly. 'What did you propose to read?'

I held up the book I had borrowed from Papa. 'This is a collection of Shakespeare – the history plays. Would you like to listen to one of them?'

He smiled then with genuine pleasure, and it lit up his wan face in spite of the fever. 'In one of my father's churches in Norfolk, in the chancel floor, there is the tomb of a knight, Sir William Calthorpe, who died in 1420. When I was a child I thought he must have died at Agincourt, and been returned to be interred in the floor of our village church. I learnt eventually that he was too old to have fought at Agincourt, although his son may have done. But his tomb was the reason I first read *Henry V*. Is it in your book?'

'Yes. Is that what you would like me to read?'

'Please. If you would.'

He settled back against his pillow, the ghost of a smile still playing on his lips. I noticed that he must have been using the almond oil, for they did not look as rough today.

Warmed by the glow of his enthusiasm, I leafed through the pages until I found the play. 'SCENE,—*At the beginning of the Play, lies in ENGLAND, but afterwards wholly in FRANCE. Enter* Chorus,' I began.

> '*O for a Muse of fire, that would ascend*
> *The brightest heaven of invention!*
> *A kingdom for a stage, princes to act,*
> *And monarchs to behold the swelling scene!*
> *Then should the warlike Harry, like himself,*

I read up to the beginning of Scene II, and looked up. Horace's eyes were closed. 'Are you asleep?' I asked softly.

'No,' he replied, 'but I feel as though I could sleep.' He lifted his soft eyes; once again, I found myself thinking that I could not possibly conceive of Horace Nelson looking licentious. It would be like St John the Evangelist looking wicked. 'Will you come again tomorrow, and read Scene II?'

'Of course I will.'

'Tomorrow should be one of my good days… but I would still enjoy listening to you read.'

'Very well, then. Shall I come again in the morning, or would another time be better?'

'Come in the afternoon. I imagine I might be grateful for a rest by then, and I can lie down and listen.'

Having set our next meeting I bade him good afternoon and left the sick berth. Tobias was lounging against one of the gun carriages with his sketchbook.

'Bravo, little sister. You still read as though you were intended for the stage,' he said, but without his usual teasing tone.

I joined him on the floor and took the sketchbook from his hand. There was a well-executed drawing of warlike Harry on his charger, surrounded by guidons, horse-guards, and swordsmen. But there were also several unsettling sketches of dark, faceless figures consumed by shadows. I flipped back through the book, but all the other drawings were in Tobias' draughtsman-like, Dürer-esque style. I turned back to the uncanny drawings.

'These are… strange, Tobias. I'm not sure that I like them; they're a little scary. Are you feeling alright?'

'Actually… not really. My head is aching, and there's a strange taste in my mouth.' He took the sketchbook back from me and examined the drawings. 'I must have been half-asleep when I made these sketches, because I don't remember doing it. I was listening to you read *Henry V* and drawing Henry going into battle, then I woke up a few minutes ago hearing you and Horace saying goodbye. My sketchbook and the charcoal were still in my hands, and these drawings were here.' He grimaced. 'They're rather horrid, aren't they?'

I searched his face. 'I hope you are not getting sick, too. Can you get up? I'll walk back to your cabin with you.'

He rose a little shakily, then shook his head. 'I just feel rather queer. As though I've had too much to drink and woke up with a sore head.'

'Since it is only mid-day, and I know you did not drink spirits at breakfast, perhaps you should go and lie down for a while,' I suggested, linking my arm in his. It would look as though we were strolling together, but I would know immediately if he stumbled or felt faint. 'Perhaps it is the heat. Is it possible you were having a nightmare, but you were not completely asleep and drew what you saw in your dream?'

'I suppose it is possible, but I've never done anything like that before. It's not a reassuring idea, Annie.'

'I did not intend it to be.'

I left him at the cabin he shared with my father and went to the wardroom to look for Papa. He was sitting at the table with his books and papers, and I explained what had happened to Tobias, but I didn't mention the unsettling sketches. I told him that Midshipman Nelson appeared to be very pleased to listen to me read to him, and that we had begun with *Henry V*. Then Papa went to look in on Tobias, Mama and I worked together on a new gown we were stitching for me, and I forgot about the strange incident of the drawings. It did not occur to me that they might come back to haunt us.

PART II

Tobias slept for most of the day. He got up for dinner, but he was silent and strange, and he disappeared back into his cabin afterwards. By the next morning, my brother was his usual, cocky self again.

'Something I ate, probably,' he said carelessly.

Horace looked extremely pleased when I made my appearance in the sick berth that afternoon. He produced a pair of battered redware cups and a pitcher, and poured a measure for each of us.

'It's lemonade. I thought, if you were going to read aloud, your throat might get dry… I know mine would,' he said shyly.

'Thank you, that's lovely.' I smiled, and he blushed charmingly. I took a sip and tried not to look surprised when I tasted it. Navy lemonade was quite a bit sharper than the beverage we sipped in the shade on the hot afternoons at my father's house, but it was undeniably refreshing. I could get used to it.

He was looking decidedly better today. There was more colour in his face, and his hands, when they lifted his cup, didn't shake at all. When I remarked on it, he said, 'On days like this, I almost feel as though I could return to duty. But the surgeon reminds me to think about how I will feel tomorrow, and remonstrates with me not to wear myself out. The paroxysms are gradually becoming less severe; he says he will clear me to return to limited duty when they are no longer debilitating.'

'They will go away completely, will they not?'

'Over time, I understand. They tell me that it might go away and come back again, in various degrees of severity, before I recover completely.'

'Oh, but that's a trial!'

He shrugged. 'Nothing I can do but see it through.'

'Of course… I'm just sorry for you.'

'I'm still here. Some other men are not.' He settled himself in his chair, resting his elbow on the table with his chin in his hand. The sleeve of his dressing gown and the wrist band of his shirt fell back from his hand, revealing his bony wrist. 'Are you ready to begin?'

'Did you not intend to rest whilst I read?'

'I *am* resting,' he asserted.

I read up to the end of Act I, as he listened with rapt attention. Sometimes when I looked up, his eyes were closed, and at other times he seemed to be looking beyond the walls of the sick berth, as if he could see the play happening somewhere beyond the wooden wall as I read it.

I stopped by seemingly unspoken agreement. 'You read wonderfully,' he said. 'I could see it all in my head. Not as though it was on a stage, but as though I was really there.' He blinked sleepily. 'I think I might lie down for a bit now. I did not want to chance falling asleep as you read,' he said apologetically.

'That's alright. I should go; I don't like to leave Tobias cooling his heels outside for too long today. He came over all queer yesterday, and I was concerned, but he felt fine this morning. He said he must have eaten something that disagreed with him.'

'Give him my regards. It must be a comfort, having your family around you.'

'Do not tell him I said this, but I will miss Tobias when he sets up his own household. I have always been closer to him than to my sister, but she is six years older than I, and Tobias is closer to my own age.'

'There are only the three of you?'

'Yes. You said you had a tiresome older brother of your own… how many siblings do you have?'

'My mother gave birth to eleven children; she died just after Kitty was born. There are eight of us, now.'

'Eight! Heavens, whatever did your poor father do…?'

'My father is a clergyman.'

'No, I meant, how did he cope, being suddenly a widower with eight children?'

'He found places for us, those of us who were old enough. William and I got sent away to school, and Maurice, Susannah, and Anne were sent to learn a trade. My uncle Suckling had always said he would secure a place for one of us in the Royal Navy, and I wanted it to be me. Maurice and William didn't contest it, so my uncle granted my petition.'

'Do you… ever regret it?'

'No. Not once,' he said emphatically.

When I left, I looked for Tobias by the same gun carriage, but he was not there. I found him perched on the lowest step of the forward companionway, looking unhappy.

'Is something wrong? Do you feel unwell again?'

He shook his head. 'No, I don't feel unwell. I just… I meant to read,'—he held up a copy of the government's justification of the Stamp Act in the American colonies—'and I took up a spot on that shot locker over there, but I fell asleep again. I had a nasty dream about a hanged man. The nastiest part was that I think it was *me* being hanged.'

'That sounds like a sign of a guilty conscience,' I said, but without much sauce. 'That *is* unpleasant, Tobias.'

'Damn me, it's just too warm down here,' he said. 'Look, tomorrow, do you mind if I don't… I'll sit just up there on the spar deck, where I could still hear you if you were to yell. I can trust the two of you, anyway, can't I?'

'You know you can.'

'I like the fellow, Anne, and he's got to be the very definition of the word *chivalry*, in the romantic, old-fashioned sense. If he were to try anything on you, I'll eat a rat.'

'Don't worry, Tobias. We'll not serve you up any rats.'

'By Morpheus,' he groaned, 'I should never have brought it up. I'll be dreaming of *that*, next.'

When I looked in on Horace the following morning, I was dismayed to see that his apparent health of the previous day might never have been. He was huddled miserably in his cot, covered by blankets, even though as we crossed the Arabian Sea and neared the equator it seemed only to get hotter. His face was drawn and white. 'Please, come back this evening,' he implored. 'I hope I'll feel well enough by then…'

'Of course I shall. Do you need anything whilst I am here?'

He moaned softly. 'No. My stomach is sick today. There's nothing to be done for it.'

The surgeon's mate came in as I stood there. 'Good morning, miss; you come to take this boy's mind off his troubles?'

'If I can,' I said, 'but it seems there is nothing I can do just now.'

'If he don't do it naturally, we'll give him a vomit. That ought to ease him some.'

'Poor Horace,' I murmured. 'I hope you feel better shortly. I'll come back this evening.' Impulsively, I lifted his limp, bony hand and kissed his knuckles, then tucked it back beneath the blankets.

'He's too ill to be read to just now,' I told Tobias when I found him above. 'He asked me to come back again this evening. The mate came in whilst I was there; he said they'd try to make him vomit to relieve his stomach. I imagine if *you* don't care to let me see you spew, Horace would not, either.'

'It's not the most dignified thing a man can do,' Tobias replied. 'Not the most undignified, either, as far as that goes. But if I were he, I'd want to preserve as much of my dignity as possible where you were concerned, dear sister.'

'Why "where I am concerned", Tobias?'

He scratched an eyebrow. 'You're a woman, Anne.'

'Oh. You concede that now, do you?'

'Go away, you. You're too old to spank, but you might make me forget that I'm a gentleman,' he said, snatching my hat and bolting as I chased him down the deck.

I did not spend long with Horace that evening. He was a little better, but so exhausted with shivering and stomach-ache that I cut short my reading, and he did not object. 'Let's see how you feel tomorrow,' I told him consolingly.

Tobias had not come with me tonight; we'd hit a series of squalls, and he had looked distinctly uneasy at supper. The loblolly boy had been drowsing in the corner, though, so we had been adequately chaperoned.

The gun ports were closed tightly, and the lanthorn swayed as the ship ploughed through the swells. As I left, however, I thought I saw someone standing between two of the larboard guns.

'Tobias...? Did you come, after all?'

There was no answer, and when the lanthorn swung in that direction, I saw that there was no one there at all. I peered around the muzzle of the nearest gun to be certain that whoever had been there hadn't sunken to the floor, perhaps in distress, but the boards were bare.

I looked around, feeling the hair rise on the back of my neck, and shuddered. We'd enthusiastically quizzed Horace about ghost ships and sailors' shades, but I didn't really believe in haunts. I would have sworn an oath that there had been someone there a moment ago, however. Remembering Tobias' mysterious sketches made the unsettling feeling stronger; there had been something familiar about that shadow, as though I had seen one of the drawings come to life. Despite the rain, I returned aft by the upper deck.

I dreamed of kraits. Kraits in the privy in Calcutta, the little black beads of their eyes shining in the moonlight. Somehow, this became the forward seat-of-ease on *Dolphin*, and when I looked down into the hole, a krait looked back, inches from my face.

*You'll never feel its bite, and you'll be dead in four hours. Suffocated to death.*

In my dream I was running down the deck, trying to outrun the snake. I made it to our cabin, and had flung the door shut against it, collapsing on our berth, when I realised that the krait was in my skirts.

I screamed, and woke sitting bolt upright with Mama's arm around me, my breast heaving and my heart pounding.

'Anne, dear…hush, child, you are safe. You were dreaming.'

I leant against her and shuddered. 'I was being chased by a krait. It was here, in bed with us. In my petticoats.'

'Darling, you aren't wearing petticoats, so there cannot be any snakes in them,' Mama said soothingly.

I laughed shakily, but there was no humour in it. 'I shall never be able to go back to sleep now, in case I die without ever waking up again.'

My mother got up and went into the wardroom to light our candle from one of the lanthorns. As its glow touched the four walls of our cabin, the last shreds of the dream dissolved like scraps of mist. I had meant what I said, though. I didn't think I would be able to fall asleep again, not tonight.

'Let's talk a little, then,' my mother said. She set our pillows behind us, and drew me against her, cradling my head with her shoulder. 'What are you reading to Mr Nelson?'

'He chose to have me read *Henry V*. He told me about the tomb of a knight in his village church, whom he thought, when he was a child, had fought at Agincourt.'

'And had he, this knight?'

'Apparently not, but he had a son who was the right age. I only just realised; Horace said the tomb was in the chancel of one of his father's churches, so his father must be the vicar. He is one of eight children living, out of eleven. His mother died when his youngest sister was an infant.

'I asked what his father did then, meaning how did he care for so many children. But Horace misunderstood me, and said his father was a clergyman. If Tobias had been a part of the conversation, he would undoubtedly have said something to the effect of not having known that becoming a vicar endowed one with such virility.'

My mother giggled. 'Yes, I can hear your brother saying such a thing, and getting away with it, too. He never seems to give offense, somehow.' She sighed. 'I often worry that he is not suited for the role for which your father is grooming him, but Edgar assures me that Tobias knows when that sort of humour is not appropriate.

'Tobias tells me that Mr Nelson appears to be a gentleman of rather old-fashioned manners,' she continued.

'That is fair, I suppose. He went to sea when he was twelve, though. I would not expect him to be sophisticated in the manner of government ministers.'

'Twelve,' my mother murmured. 'Poor child.'

'He was disappointed to have missed you when you called on him the other day. You must come with us again soon.'

'Ask him tomorrow to choose a day and time.'

'Tomorrow will be his fever day. Perhaps the day after that. I will ask.'

We chatted inconsequentially, like girls in the schoolroom, for a while. Gradually, I forgot the terror of my dream. Mama extinguished the candle, and we both slept until dawn.


Horace looked alarming. There was a fever flush across his cheeks, and his soft eyes were hollowed and red.

'Perhaps I should not stay today. You look terribly unwell this morning,' I said quietly, taking his gaunt hand.

'Please, don't go. It isn't as bad as it must look,' he said, tightening his hand around mine. 'I didn't sleep well last night, is all. I had an evil dream. Not that kind of evil dream,' he added hastily, proving that he was not as unsophisticated as he seemed.

'So did I,' I said. 'And mine was not that kind of evil, either, but it was certainly evil. I dreamt I was pursued and bitten by a krait. It was in my petticoats. I think I screamed before I woke up. I remember screaming in the dream.' I felt myself shudder again, and he squeezed my hand. 'I was afraid to go back to sleep, in case I died in my sleep.'

'I dreamt of birds. Storm petrels, but they called to me with the voices of drowned men. I followed their voices onto the upper deck, and they were swooping and diving over the surface of the sea. They were calling to me to join them. All I had to do was throw myself over the side…' His eyes were troubled. 'I almost wanted to,' he confessed in a pained whisper.

'No…! Do not *ever* think that way,' I implored him, taking up his other hand and clasping them both tightly. 'I know things are challenging now, but you will be well again, Horace. You mustn't give in to despair. Where would England be if Henry had given up?'

'In France,' he said dryly.

'Exactly!' I clasped those thin hands between my own. 'We'd be part of France. And Britannia needs her champions, because France still wants England as her prize. You have to take that lieutenant's exam.'

'I intend to.' He tried to smile. 'Thank you, Anne. It is hard to stay cheerful when every bone in my body aches, but it will be better again tomorrow. I have to think of that.'

I released his hands and brought a chair over beside his cot. 'How strange that we both had deathly dreams on the same night. Even stranger...'

'What?'

'A couple of days ago—do you remember I said that something happened to Tobias, and we were worried he was ill? He was 'chaperoning', sitting out there against one of the gun carriages with his sketchbook. He draws very well, in a lovely classical style. He had started drawing Henry going into battle with his army, but then, he said, he sort of fell asleep. When he woke up, he'd done these horrid sketches of faceless figures consumed by shadows... darkness within darkness. Even Tobias said they were horrid. They weren't in his usual style at all, and there was a... a deeply unsettling quality to them. It certainly unsettled Tobias. He said his head ached as if he'd had too much to drink, and that there was a strange taste in his mouth. He went to bed for the rest of the day.'

Horace frowned. 'He didn't remember drawing them?'

'No. Then the following day—he'd woken feeling like himself again, but he was sitting out there on one of the shot lockers, reading some tedious government opinion, and he fell asleep again. But this time, he dreamt he was being hanged.

'That was the day before yesterday. I didn't ask Tobias if he dreamt anything last night, but you and I both did.

'The other odd thing is that last night, as I was leaving, I thought there was someone standing between the two guns on the larboard side, but when the lanthorn swung in that direction, there was no one there at all. But for a moment, it struck me that I was seeing one of Tobias' sketches come to life.'

'You should have come back inside the sick berth. You might have been in danger.'

'In danger from what? There was no one—nothing—there. I went aft on the upper deck, rather than the gun deck, just the same,' I confessed.

He tried to push himself upright in his cot. I helped him arrange the pillow to support his back. I could see how even this required a terrific effort from him, and I remembered my father's softly spoken assessment: *I hope he makes it home.*

'Can I bring you something to drink, Horace?'

'That's kind of you; thank you.' I filled his mug from the pitcher, which only contained water this day. 'I don't know how much I believe in all those superstitions I told you about,' he said, accepting the mug from me, 'but it seems to me that there are far too many conjunctions amongst these occurrences to call them coincidence.' He sipped some water cautiously. 'I'd rather not vomit any more if I can help it,' he explained, 'so I shall have to drink it slowly.'

I felt myself frown sympathetically, but he wasn't watching me. 'There is a sailor who brings my meals and things; he sleeps here at night when I'm very unwell. Bart was here last night; when I see him next I shall ask him if he dreamt anything unpleasant,' he said, before taking another slow sip.

'If he did, what would that tell us?'

'I have no idea,' Horace admitted.

I read a bit more from *Henry V* as he drank his water, but I could see his strength was flagging. When the mug was empty I took it from him and set it on the table.

'You need to sleep. You must make up for your disturbed rest last night.' I brushed away a lock of hair that was stuck to his damp brow. 'Don't think too hard about our strange mystery, and try not to dream.'

'Come back tomorrow,' he murmured, his eyes closing. 'We can try to work it out then.'

I had forgotten to ask Horace when I might bring my mother to meet him, but, as I told her, 'It isn't as though he'll not be at home, and today he is less likely to be indisposed.' When I spoke to him through the canvas bulkhead and told him that Mama was with me, his voice said, 'Give me a moment,' and I heard him rustling through the chest underneath his cot.

'Come in,' he called.

He was standing to greet us, with his dressing gown neatly arranged, and I saw that he had brushed his hair. It still grew every which way, and it needed trimming, but I was touched that he had tried to tame it a little.

'Mrs Middleton,' he said, extending his hand. My mother offered her hand, and he bowed low over it. At that moment, pale, wasted Horace could have held his own at a Governor's Reception.

'I am very pleased to make your acquaintance at last, Mr Nelson,' Mama said. 'My family has spoken warmly of you.'

'I hope I merit their kind opinions,' he replied, bringing a chair for my mother. He moved carefully, but he wasn't wobbly. I was pleased for him.

Once my mother was seated he brought a chair for me, and as he placed it I saw the muscles in his legs and arms shaking. I bit my lip, but I took the chair and let him collect a final one for himself. I had to stop myself from springing up when he dropped into its seat, a little less than gracefully.

'I apologise for my clumsiness,' he said. 'Anne can attest that the past two days have taken a lot out of me, but I'm much improved today.'

'Horace seemed to be getting better, but I was concerned at how severely the last paroxysm used him,' I said, with compete honesty. 'But he told me that the physicians said it might happen.'

'I saw it in Jamaica, when I was there with my husband, and Clarice, my eldest child, was just a baby, Mr Nelson. The lady was the Governor's wife, and she was a lovely woman, very accomplished, and a charming hostess, but she suffered very badly from the intermittent fever. I saw it progress, over the course of the year we were there. Some weeks she felt almost well, but then she would have a series of more severe paroxysms. But I hope you will take heart from the fact that she recovered completely, and has just been presented with her first grandson, in London.'

'I hope to be as fortunate one day, madam,' Horace said. He suddenly looked pained, and I was prepared to worry again, but he only said, 'I am sorry I cannot offer you any refreshment. I would have liked to—'

'Do not concern yourself, sir,' Mama assured him. 'I shall not stay long, and I did not expect to take refreshment, as we shall have our mid-day meal before long. But I wanted to meet the young gentleman of whom all my family speaks well.'

'You do me too much honour,' he murmured, and I wondered if Mama was not laying it on a little thick.

'Mama went to Jamaica when she was only Tobias' age,' I volunteered.

'I have been to Jamaica,' Horace said. 'I went there on a merchant ship when I was thirteen. That trip taught me much about how to be a sailor.' I looked at him with some surprise. He had not spoken of this to me.

'I understand you are studying to become a lieutenant?'

'I am, although one cannot—technically—become a lieutenant until the age of twenty. I will be eighteen in September. I am hoping that they will let me stand for the exam early.'

'Do I detect a hint of the northeast in your speech, Mr Nelson?' Mama asked. 'Where do you hail from?'

'Norfolk, madam. The village of Burnham Thorpe, Kings Lynn.' He looked wistful. 'I have been to the West Indies, and to the Arctic; I have navigated the Medway and the Thames, and now I have seen the East Indies, but Burnham will always be my home. Have you ever been there?' he asked hopefully.

'No; I'm afraid the closest I have been is Cambridge. But Anne tells me that you have a knight of Agincourt in the crypt of your village church…'

'He is actually under the chancel floor, and I do not believe now that he actually fought at Agincourt, but when I was young I imagined that he had. I used to invent adventures for him. My mother is buried to the right of him.' His voice dropped, and he sounded unintentionally sad.

'I understand she died when you were quite young. I am very sorry,' my mother said.

'God rest her,' Horace said. 'I hope she would be proud of me.'

'I am sure that she is,' I interjected. 'Who would not be? You did not tell me you have done all these things, and you are not yet eighteen! What will you do in the next thirty years, Horace Nelson?'

He smiled at me then. 'I believe I shall be defending Britannia from the predations of France,' he said.

My mother rose, and Horace stood quickly. 'I shall be going, Mr Nelson, but I must agree with my daughter: I am sure your mother would be very proud of you. What is her name, that I might say a prayer tonight for her?'

'Catherine, madam.'

'Ah, that is my name, too, so I shall not forget it.' She inclined her head. 'Be well, dear sir. When you are recovered, I hope you will take tea with us. Anne, dear, I will see you at dinner.'

She departed, and Horace and I returned to our seats. 'I was almost afraid that you would do yourself an injury being chivalrous,' I said. 'But you made a good impression.'

He tried to look indignant, but failed. 'I was a little afraid that I might have overreached myself,' he admitted. 'You saw my muscles shaking, didn't you?'

'Yes. Be assured that either one of us would have been quick to catch you if you collapsed. But I hoped you would not. It would have changed the tone of the visit considerably.'

'Another lesson in humility, if I needed one.'

'Wot is?' said a voice. A man came into the sick berth, depositing a tray containing a wooden bowl of stew and a piece of soft bread, spread thickly with butter, on the table. 'Din't know yeh were entertainin', sir. I brung your dinner. It's mutton, wi' onions and… wegetables. Hullo, miss.'

'Anne, this is Bart. I told you about him.'

'Yes; I'm pleased to make your acquaintance, Mr Bart.'

'Jest Bart, miss; an' likewise. It's Bart-olomew, really, but I gets tired of hexplainin' that it in't said like th' *"th"* in "thump".'

Bart pulled up a stool. 'Yeh need to eat this, afore it gets cold, sir. That's if the lady don't mind.'

'I do not mind; Horace, please eat it while it is warm. I'll come back this afternoon, if you like.'

'Wait, Anne. I asked Bart whether he dreamt last night. What he told me was interesting. Will you tell it again, Bart?'

'It in't somethin' I'd ordinarily tell a lady, sir,' Bart said slowly. 'But…if yeh really want me to… I had a dream last night that I was dyin' of th' Black Lion… th' French disease. Me nose fell off… 'mongst… other bits.' He rubbed his nose, as if to ensure that it was still attached to his face. 'I took care of a feller once't who died of it, and it were right 'orrible. And 'im an orfficer, too. In Indonesia, that were, and there weren't a chance o' gettin' 'im 'ome, 'e rotted so farst.'

'Ugh. I don't know how that won't put you off your food, Horace, but you are the one who asked him to repeat it.' I had some idea of what the French disease was, or at least, how a person got it. It was one of the educational perquisites of having Tobias as a sibling. 'That must have been a horrifying dream, Bart.'

'As bad as yours, or mine,' Horace said. 'We seem to all be dreaming about things that terrify us.'

'Why, though?'

'That,' said Horace, picking up his spoon, 'is what we need to find out.'


I did not return that afternoon, however, because we sailed into a storm, one bad enough to keep us to our cabins as *Dolphin* pitched and rolled. It was an unnerving feeling, as she rose on the crests and sank in the troughs, but it didn't make me or my parents ill. In contrast, I could hear poor Tobias being repeatedly sick over the chamber pot, in the cabin he shared with our father, for most of the evening and into the night. Curious how he and Reecy were subject to being seasick, but the rest of us were not. I was sure that he would not have found it at all interesting in his current condition, however.

I was also not inclined to thank him for his assertion that if you met the *Flying Dutchman* in a storm, you would go to the bottom with her.

It was not until early afternoon on the following day that I made my way back to the sick berth. The sea was returning to a more reasonable state, but I was nevertheless required to lurch from gun breech to gun breech in the semi-darkness, in response to *Dolphin*'s motion. The sun was beginning to reappear in the sky above, but with the gunports closed, and only enough lanthorns alight to be able to check that the ropes securing the gun carriages were secure, it was still quite dark. I could see the light from the lanthorns in the sick berth shining on the canvas ahead, though, so it helped keep me on course. The galley was cold and deserted, although they'd surely relight the galley fire shortly, now that the sea was calming.

I mistimed my progress from one gun to the next against the roll of the ship, and barked my shin sharply on a gun carriage, causing myself to land on the decking on my knees. I rearranged my skirts to examine my ankle. My stocking was intact, and there was no evidence of blood, but I was certain that there would be an ugly bruise there. I started to get up, supporting myself on the gun, prepared to launch myself again when I felt the hair rise on the back of my neck.

It was inexplicable. Apart from the moving shadows caused by the swinging lanthorns, there was no reason for the sensation that swept over me and caused me to flee the rest of the length of the deck, bouncing off the cascabels of more than one gun. It was the same blind panic from my dream of being chased by the krait.

I was that sense of terror that made me fling myself into the light and safety of the sick berth without announcing myself first.

I was not intruding upon Horace's privacy, however. He was lying flat in his cot, smothered in blankets, and so still that I was not sure he was breathing.

I got my own breath under control before whispering his name.

'Horace?' I crept nearer to the cot. 'Are you awake?'

He *was* apparently breathing, but I had never seen him look so lifeless, even on his worst fever day. His skin was stretched thinly across his cheekbones, and his eyelids looked transparent, so blue that I fancied I was seeing his eyes through the skin. His lower lip was badly chapped again, cracked and bleeding. I glanced around for the pot of sweet almond oil, but I did not see it.

'Horace?' I asked again. I was not sure why I did not just leave him to sleep, except that he was alone in the sick berth once again, and I was still unnerved by my flight down the gun deck. It was both of those things, combined with his unnatural stillness, that made me lay my hand on the crown of his head. I might have taken his hand, but both of them were concealed beneath the blankets.

He opened his eyes slowly, and responded with a wan smile when he saw me. 'Anne,' he said. I waited, but he didn't say anything more.

'Hello,' I responded. 'That was quite a storm, wasn't it?'

'I've seen worse,' he murmured. 'But it was bad enough.'

'My poor brother probably hopes never to see another like it.'

'Tell him I sympathise.' He closed his eyes again briefly. 'Tobias is not the only person who suffers from seasickness.'

'Oh. Poor Horace; is that why you look so dreadful?'

'Fair to say.'

'Is it over, now?'

'It seems to be,' he said faintly. 'I still have to deal with the ague today, though.' His breath was sour.

'You look as though you ought to drink something. And your lip is bleeding.'

He touched his lip and regarded the tips of his fingers disinterestedly. 'There is a jug over there on the table. Pour me a little of that. Your little pot of emollient is in my chest.'

I poured a small amount of the liquid into a cup. It smelt of ginger and mint. He struggled into a more vertical position, and extended a hand that trembled so badly I was afraid he might spill it, little of it as there was. 'Let me help.' I held the cup, his fingers guiding mine. They felt unnaturally cold.

I held it steady as he sipped cautiously, until he indicated he was finished. 'Give me a few minutes to see how it sits.'

I moved a spotlessly clean basin off the top of his trunk and undid the latch. His dressing gown lay crumpled atop everything else, but the pot of almond oil was just underneath. I extracted a dab with my finger and applied it gingerly to his bottom lip.

'Tell me if I'm hurting you.'

His mouth twitched. 'You can press harder than that. I promise I shall not bite you.'

I stroked my finger along the contour of his ravaged lip, distributing the emollient evenly. He had a full lower lip that bowed slightly in the middle. Blonde bristles adorning his upper lip kept his mouth from appearing feminine, but it was a very sensitive-looking mouth. He needed a shave. I realised what I was doing, analysing his face, and blushed. Thankfully his

*(doe-like...)*

eyes were closed at that moment, so I don't think he noticed. 'Is that better?' I asked, retreating a slight distance.

He nodded minutely.

'Tell me, did you dream anything last night?' I continued, trying to direct my thoughts away from Mr Nelson's lips.

'I did not sleep last night,' he murmured. 'I could not possibly have dreamt.'

'Oh. No, I suppose you would not have. I didn't sleep, either. I wonder if anyone did.' I filled the cup again and offered it to him.

He took it from me and rested it on his breastbone between sips. His hand still shook, but it did not seem as bad as I'd first thought. 'If we are to collect more empirical evidence, we will have to find out if the dreams reoccur, or if we experience… other… disturbing dreams,' he said.

'I'd really rather not. But you are right. We need to approach them analytically, instead of emotionally.' I recounted to him what had happened to me on the gundeck earlier. Hearing the cook firing up the galley stove, banging the grates and seeing to the boiling-vats, my fear seemed childish; at the time, it had been very real.

'And you saw no one?'

'Not even a shadow. I cannot tell you what frightened me so badly. It was completely irrational.'

I read to Horace from *Henry V* for a while, and the surgeon's mate came and spoke to him, assuring that he was not in any desperate need. I thought he looked a little better when I left. In the afternoon light, with the clatter of the cook in the galley and the activity of the ship all around, dreams seemed of no consequence. But I was almost dreading the night.

None of us dreamt that night, though, nor for any of the following nights. Midshipman Nelson was getting stronger, and although his clothes still hung on him like shirts on a washing line, his eyes were brighter and he had more stamina. I finished reading *Henry V*, and after we concluded the dark tale of *Richard III,* we decided not to begin another play.

On the morning that he was to move out of the sick berth and into the midshipmen's berth on the orlop, Tobias and I arranged to breakfast with him, and we dined on eggs and freshly-caught fish with mushroom catsup.

Horace was resplendent in his midshipman's uniform, even if it looked as though had been made for a larger man.

'What will your duties be?' Tobias asked.

'Not much,' he admitted. 'I am to keep maintaining my journal, and plotting navigation, and I may stand a day watch every few days. But I'll not be going aloft, nor will I be responsible for a division of men. I believe I am to continue studying, for the most part.' He chased a bit of fish around his plate. 'The surgeon has warned me that I may yet end up back here again before this passage is over.'

'I sincerely hope *not*,' I exclaimed.

'We all know it is the nature of my illness,' Horace said simply. 'But I do hope not, myself.'

'You are still requested to have tea with our family one afternoon,' I reminded him.

'I look forward to it, with pleasure.'

'We have the use of the wardroom,' Tobias informed him, 'and you must come as my guest, whenever you like, and converse with Anne and me.'

Horace pushed back his chair and rose. 'You are both so good and kind to me. I am exceedingly glad you are aboard. The past weeks would have been wretched without you.' He straightened his coat. Picking up his hat, he bowed. 'And now, I must go attend to the relocation of my sea chest.'

We watched him depart, his slight figure weaving through the early-morning activity of the gun deck. 'I think we had best keep a close eye on him,' Tobias said soberly. 'I do not think he's out of the weeds, yet.'

We went above to take the air before the day became hot. Mr Tremaine tipped his hat to me, a confident smile lighting his eyes. He was certainly handsome, I conceded, with his dark hair and eyes and golden complexion. He was about Tobias' age, but he and Tobias seemed to circle around one another like wary cats. *Too much alike*, I thought.

I didn't speak to Mr Nelson again for two or three days. I came across him sitting on deck with his journal in the evening after supper. He was not writing, however, but was gazing out over the sea. Somewhere out there, off our starboard bow, was the coast of Africa.

'Anne,' he said, smiling. He stood up from the box he'd been occupying, and offered it to me.

'It's good to see you,' I said, accepting his seat. 'Tell me, how has your return to duty been?'

He settled himself on the ground opposite me. The sun was still high, warming his pale skin.

He looked well, apart from the blue smudges, like bruises, on the fragile skin under his eyes. 'It is going well,' he said. 'Although I tire so easily, I'm utterly fagged when I drop into my hammock at night. My messmates have embraced me as one of them, although Mr Tremaine was disappointed to discover that I shall not be relieving him of any of his watches.'

'He always tips his hat to me,' I volunteered.

'He seems an agreeable fellow. I have not gotten to know any of them yet, really.' He looked pleased. 'Today was my fever day, and I was able to work through it! Either the paroxysms are weakening, or I am getting used to them; I hardly minded it.'

'That's very encouraging, Horace! You must be getting stronger, too.'

'I think so. I feel stronger.'

'You must tell us when you are at leisure to come to tea with us. My parents will be delighted to see you looking so well.'

'I could do it the day after tomorrow, I think,' he said, consulting his journal. 'Yes. Tomorrow I am on watch during the first dog, but the day after I am free at that time.'

'Then you *are* standing watches—!'

He chuckled ironically. 'Only the dog watches, and only four times a week. It's hardly any wonder that Mr Tremaine was disappointed. Still, the fellows that I relieve for two hours are plenty happy to have them.'

'I confess, Horace, that I have missed talking to you. It had become a portion of my day that I looked forward to.'

'Not nearly as much as I did, I imagine. I have missed our conversations, too. I hope you have had no more bad dreams…?'

'None. At least, none that I remember, so if I did they must not have been *very* bad. Have you?'

'I do not think I've dreamt at all since I moved into the midshipmen's berth. It is not as amiable as the sick berth, being in the orlop, but I do not think it matters. At the end of the day, I think I could fall asleep in the hold.'

'Remembering what you told me about snakes the day I met you, I hope you will never have to sleep in the hold,' I exclaimed.

'I said something about snakes in the hold?'

'I said there are no snakes on a ship, and you said they might come in with the cargo.'

He looked bewildered. 'I honestly do not remember saying that. Knowing now how you fear them, I hope I would not be so ungentlemanly.'

'You were not at your best. You have always been a perfect gentleman, Horace.'

He hesitated. 'Perhaps… we could continue our conversation when my schedule allows? That is, if you want to.'

'Yes! …I mean, I would find that very agreeable.'

'Well! Then I will seek you out, when I have some time free.'

The master's mate appeared on deck. 'Mr Nelson! A word, please.'

'I hope I have not caused you trouble, just now,' I said.

'I doubt it. I am not under any obligation, at the moment. I imagine he just wants to see me about some figures I submitted to him.' He rose and straightened his jacket. It looked as if it fitted him better than it had a few days before, even if physically he seemed much the same. 'I will see you tomorrow, Anne.'

'Good evening, Horace. Sleep well.'

Tea with my parents was an amiable success, and every other day, give or take, we spent an agreeable hour in conversation. Tobias, who hadn't touched his sketchbook since the strange incident on the gun deck, got it out again one afternoon, when the three of us sat and sketched one another. Horace, who turned out to be a competent draughtsman, did a flattering sketch of me, and Tobias captured Horace leaning against the stern rail, laughing. My sketch of Horace, of his face as he studied his drawing, was not as successful. With his downcast eyes, he looked as though he were sleeping. I much preferred the liveliness of Tobias' drawing.

As we sailed south, the weather became more temperate. It would begin to get hot again after we rounded the Cape of Good Hope and approached the equator again.

Horace's health wavered, but held. 'Some days are better than others,' he admitted. Still, nothing was bad enough to send him back to the sick berth.

We picked up fresh produce off Cape Town, and rejoiced in salad, fruit, and fresh beef for a week.

One morning, at the start of the forenoon watch, I found Horace sitting in the light of an open gun port, in his waistcoat and shirt-sleeves, mending his coat.

'Accident with a fork,' he said shortly.

'How did you tear your coat with a fork?' I asked.

'I did not say *I* tore it.' He held up his left arm, which had been underneath the sleeve he was trying to repair. His shirt sleeve was pushed up, and there was a strip of bandage wrapped around his thin forearm from his wrist to four inches below his elbow.

'Good heavens — what happened?!'

'It was a mouse.'

'A mouse with a fork?'

He glanced up from his work, with a look that said he did not share my humour. 'No, Mr Tremaine had the fork. He was trying to spear the mouse. My arm happened to be in the way.'

I grimaced. 'He was trying to spear a mouse with a fork?' *What gruesome sport!*

'We think it must have come aboard in the crate of oranges my mess bought from those bumboats off Cape Town. Mr Tremaine found it in his sea chest nibbling on his bag of macadamia nuts.'

He set down the coat, and I could see two parallel tears in the sleeve. 'The mouse ran up the table leg, where I was trying to study. It ran right across my book, and my wrist. I did not move my arm fast enough.'

'That's terrible, Horace! Did he hurt you badly?'

'He did not impale me, don't worry. It is only a couple of deep scratches. As I said, it was an accident. He apologised profusely.'

'It must hurt, though.'

'It does, rather.' He raised his head and met my eyes, and I saw the effects of the ordeal in the pallor of his face. 'Not as bad as it did when the surgeon poured spirits of wine on it to disinfect the wounds, though.'

'I am so sorry.'

'Why? *You* did not stab me with a fork.'

'May the heavens strike me dead if I ever do anything to hurt you!'

He smiled then. 'Anne,' he said, 'I know you would not.'

But as the weather grew hotter again, Horace grew limper. He confessed that his energy frequently deserted him by mid-afternoon, but he still continued to fag through the rest of the day.

We lounged on the aft part of the deck in the early evening, too hot to say much. We had been at sea for close to three months now, halfway through the long haul.

The ship was on a larboard tack, and the main topsail cast a welcome shadow over the stern. I stirred the air with my folding fan, turning to Horace and directing a thin breeze across the shock of hair plastered to his brow beneath his hat.

'Thank you,' he said, without opening his eyes. 'I was not sure I would be able to make it through, this afternoon. At one point when I was on watch I thought I might faint.'

I stopped fanning. 'Why did you not tell the lieutenant?'

'I didn't faint.'

'Horace…'

'It passed, Anne. I think it was just… I could not sleep, last night. Something unsettled me.'

'Do you have any idea what it was?'

He sat up, bracing his back against the stern. 'I have an idea… but it does not make sense. It's too fanciful.'

'Tell me.'

He lowered his voice, even though no one was nearby. 'You know that relations between Mr Tremaine and myself have been a bit strained since the incident with the fork. Last night, he tried to make amends, of a sort… he was talking about a statue that he'd purchased at a bazaar, something he seemed quite proud of. It was reputed to have come from some ancient fortress and temple complex in the interior. He claims it can give power to its owner, and grant wishes.

'He took the thing out of his sea chest. It was wrapped in a patterned handkerchief, and when he unwrapped it, I felt my skin crawl. I handed it to me, and I am not even sure why I took it, because it repulsed me.'

He found his own handkerchief and wiped the sweat from his face. 'It was only about five inches high, made of bronze, I think; I'm not sure. Just a little figure of a man, dancing… but it was obscene.'

He saw the expression on my face and said, 'Not obscene like that; it wore some sort of clout around its loins and its … erm… manhood… was completely covered.' I could not tell if he was blushing, or if he was just flushed from the heat of the day. 'When I say it was obscene, I'm only describing the feeling I got from it.

'Apart from the clout, it wore nothing but some wide cuffs on its wrists, but there was a crown of flames sculpted around its head. And its eyes were set with amber stones, which made it look as though there was a fire burning inside it.'

He shuddered, and I thought he looked more unwell than he had in weeks. 'I could hardly contain my revulsion, but I did not want to offend Mr Tremaine. I feigned an interest in it while he talked of ancient Muslim energies, but I really could not wait to give the unholy thing back. Afterwards, I felt rather unwell and went to bed, but I slept very badly. I kept startling awake, feeling as though there was something dangerous close by… watching me.'

He had been staring at his hands, now he looked up at me, and his eyes were troubled. 'It is only an ugly bronze statue. I'm investing an inanimate object with a malevolent energy. It bothers me that it affected me so profoundly.'

'It sounds truly horrid. But I am more concerned about you than about an ugly heathen statue, Horace.'

'I am fine, Anne,' he said listlessly. 'It is just the heat.'

That night, I had the dream again. I opened my eyes, and looked directly into the inquisitive black eyes of the krait. It didn't look at all malicious as it bit me, and I did not feel its fangs, but I couldn't breathe, and I knew its venom was paralysing my lungs. I woke gasping, and as soon as I realised that I was awake and I was *not* suffocating, I slipped out of our berth and tossed a cotton shawl over my nightdress, then escaped to the spar deck.

As I came on deck, I saw a slight figure in shirtsleeves standing at the rail in the light of a waxing moon, a long queue trailing down his back between his shoulder blades, and his mop of crazy hair standing up every which way.

'Horace…?' I whispered. For a moment, I was unsure whether I was seeing Midshipman Nelson, or a spectre assuming his shape.

I crept a little closer. 'Horace?' I said, slightly louder.

He turned then, and I could see that he was not a dream or projection. But his eyes in the moonlight looked huge and distressed. 'Anne.' He took my hand, and I could feel *his* shaking.

'Did it come back? Your dream?' I asked softly.

He nodded. 'Except this time, in the dream, I actually did it. I actually went over the side.' His voice quavered.

I instinctively drew him away from the rail. I almost said something blasphemous, but if he was not going to, neither would I. 'Come and sit with me,' I entreated him.

We found a place in the bow against the starboard 3-pounder, and sat with our backs against the carriage. Horace rested his arms on his knees and hung his head.

We did not speak for some time.

'What would your father say, if you told him this?' I asked, eventually.

'I suppose my father would acknowledge the presence of evil in the world, but would likely tell me that I am stronger than that,' he said, slowly. 'That the protection of my baptism keeps me safe from real harm.' He swallowed. 'What would yours say?'

'I'm not sure I'd know what to tell him, to begin with,' I confessed. 'He would probably say that dreams cannot hurt me. And that the only power a statue can have is the power that we ascribe to it.'

He didn't say anything immediately. When he finally replied, he said, 'The thing that's bothering me is that I did not ascribe any power to that object. I feel as though it *took* it from me.'

I began to consider the impossibility of this, but my thoughts were interrupted by the clatter of feet on the companionway. A figure staggered for the side, and I heard him gag, then retch. By now I could identify Tobias' retching in a howling storm. It was unmistakable on a still, clear night.

I got to my feet and walked down the deck to him. He straightened, wiping his mouth on his nightshirt sleeve.

'Tobias. Are you alright now…?'

He took a few heaving breaths, then nodded.

'Horace and I are down by the beakhead. Come and sit with us.'

'What… what are you doing in the middle of the night… out here with Horace, little sister?' His voice didn't sound much steadier than Horace's had.

'Neither of us could sleep. And we're hardly going to attempt anything improper on deck, under the eyes of the watch, even were we inclined that way, dear brother.'

Tobias sank down on the deck beside us. 'Ate something at supper that disagreed with you?' Horace asked mildly.

Tobias shook his head, whether to answer in the negative or to clear it, I couldn't tell. 'That's the first time I've ever had a *dream* that made me puke.'

'Do you want to talk about it?'

'No. Yes. Damn me, I don't know!'

'Was it the same dream you had before, Tobias?' I asked carefully.

His shoulders drooped. 'Yes. Only this time, I was on the scaffold, and the bloody trap-door opened, and I *dropped*. I woke up choking.' He scrubbed both of his hands down his face. 'I had to get out of there before I woke up Papa.'

I took his hand. 'I dreamt that I was bitten by a krait, and was suffocating.'

'And I dreamt that I drowned,' Horace said.

Tobias looked at both of us. 'Tonight?'

We both nodded.

'This is… this is not… it doesn't make sense.' He looked from Horace to me. 'Have you had these dreams before?'

'Yes. But the first time, the thing we feared did not actually *happen*.' Horace looked ghastly in the moonlight, his eyes deep in shadow. His face had begun to fill out again, but his cheekbones were still prominent; in this light it looked as though his skin had become transparent and we were seeing the skull beneath.

'Is this… is there one of your sailor's myths that explains this? One that you didn't tell us about?' Tobias' voice sounded both accusing and hopeful at the same time.

'Not that I know of. I don't think this is any myth. But I don't know what it is.'

'Shit,' Tobias whispered. He never used that vulgarity, so I knew he must be really rattled.

We stayed there, with me between the two boys, for the rest of the night, and at some point I fell asleep again with my head in one of their laps. I don't actually know whose it was.


The reason I don't know which boy's lap I slept in was because I was both dropped and lifted at the same time, so that I came fully awake standing in front of the first lieutenant. Tobias and Horace were standing behind me, and I think each one of them had a hand under one of my arms. I could feel Horace trembling on my right.

'Relax, children. You are not in trouble. We are going to change tacks, and I need Mr Nelson, because he is going to direct it. Mr and Miss Middleton, I suggest you relocate to someplace away from the lines. If you wish to observe from a point behind the wheel, you are welcome. Mr Nelson, please follow me.'

I watched Horace stumble in his shirtsleeves after the lieutenant, and I was not sure I believed him that Horace was not about to be reprimanded. 'He woke Horace up from a dead sleep, and wants him to tack?' I said to Tobias.

'He hardly looks as though he remembers his own name,' Tobias muttered. 'I don't think this will go well.'

We followed at a distance, and took up a position respectably removed from the action. I was too much aware that Tobias and I were in our nightclothes, but no one was observing *us*.

Horace was handed a speaking cone, and was told to tack when ready. I watched him swallow hard, and look from the master's mate at the wheel, to the men on the lines and tops. I saw him shiver, and I could not tell if it was from nerves or ague. Then he lifted his chest, drew back his shoulders, and lifted the speaking cone.

His voice was thin, and it broke a little with effort, but he gave the commands in a steady, clear voice. 'Stand by to come about…'

I saw the crew ready the lines, waiting for the next command.

'Ease down the helm,' he shouted. The master's mate eased the wheel until it was hard over. I saw Horace take a deep breath. He seemed to hold it for a moment, then cried, 'Ease headsail sheets!'

The sheets were eased until the sails were backed, completely spilling their wind. This was where the timing was critical; if she didn't catch the wind on this new tack, she'd be stopped dead. Horace shouted, 'Mainsail haul!'

I watched the yards come around, and I saw Horace hesitate. A look of panic flickered in his eyes, then he bellowed 'Tack down the sprit yard…!' His voice cracked. 'Let go and haul!!'

I watched the fore yards begin to fill. 'Pass fore and aft,' he croaked.

He'd done it. *Dolphin* had not missed stays.

I had not realised I'd been holding my breath. I released it as Horace dropped the speaking cone to his side.

The lieutenant laid a hand on Horace's left shoulder and shook his right hand, congratulating him on a successful tack. I saw Horace nod, and the master's mate patted him heartily on the back. The other midshipmen came to shake his hand, or pound his back, or both.

As the last one punched his arm before heading back to his duties, Horace turned to me and Tobias. He smiled uncertainly, and I clasped my hands together in a gesture of congratulations as he started to walk towards us. I quickly dropped them again, however, as Horace sank gracefully to the deck, Tobias darting out to catch him before his head connected with the boards.


'Do you dislike us so very much, then,' the surgeon asked, 'that you would not come to us when the paroxysms began to grow stronger again?'

'They were not so bad that I could not perform my duties,' Horace mumbled. 'They are light enough…' Tobias and I sat either side of him in the sick berth, for emotional support more than anything else. He was shivering with ague again.

The surgeon gave him as blanket, and we helped him wrap it around his shoulders. 'I am tempted to have you reassigned to the sick berth,' the surgeon chided Horace sternly.

'Please, sir. The p-paroxysms are not that bad,' Horace pleaded, obviously trying to keep his teeth from chattering. His voice was a ragged whisper. 'It just took me off guard this morning. I did not even notice it when we were tacking. It was only afterwards that it caught up to me.'

'I will delay making a decision until I have had some time to observe you. I would like you to stay here in the sick berth for the remainder of today, and all day tomorrow, so I can judge the severity of your symptoms. If I determine that they are not dangerous, I will not have you transferred back.'

'Do you want me to get anything from your sea chest?' Tobias asked, as the surgeon departed, having consigned Horace to his old cot.

'M-my journal… and my lieutenant's exam book. P-pen and ink. I h-hope I won't be here for more than the t-t-two days.'

I stayed whilst he removed his coat, waistcoat, and shoes, and climbed into the cot. I smoothed the sheet and blanket, and tucked them in around him as he sank into the pillow. 'Humility,' he muttered.

'You did wonderfully well, Horace, particularly with the lieutenant having surprised you like that. Tobias and I were afraid you'd get confused, or would not be able to remember the orders.'

'I nearly did. Somehow I managed to pull the right command out of my head,' he croaked. 'Would you find me something to drink, please, Anne? My throat is raw from shouting.'

Bart had brought him a jug of orange whey, which was sweet and mildly cooling, for his throat. I poured some into a cup and held it for him to sip. 'Anne, it is so discouraging to be back here.' I tried not to notice that he was fighting back tears.

'It's only for a little while. Two nights, and a day and a half. Then you'll be back in your hot, dark, smelly, cave-like midshipmen's berth with the mice and the forks and th...' My voice trailed off. I didn't want him to think about the evil little statue.

I don't think he was thinking of it. He laughed weakly, which made him cough, and I helped him sip some more whey. His eyes were drifting closed, and he kept forcing them open again.

'You want to sleep,' I observed. 'I'll go, but I can come back later, if you like.'

'Yes,' he murmured, 'please. I only need a bit of rest...'

Tobias came back with Horace's journal, book, and writing box, and we left them on the table for him when he woke up.

Sleeping on deck against a gun carriage is not the best of accommodations, and I was happy to take advantage of the berth in our cabin for a nap after breakfast. Mama professed that she had not been terribly worried when she and Papa awoke and found Tobias and me gone. 'There are only so many places the two of you might have gone, and we would have known had you gone overboard, if the watch was doing its job.'

I thought of Horace's dream and suppressed a shudder. None of us had dreamed again, last night. I hoped our sleep would be dreamless for a long time.

We went back to the sick berth late that afternoon, Tobias and I, but Horace was still sick and shivering and apologetic, and we told him we would come again in the morning. 'If you want to get out of here quickly, you can't have us hanging about. Try to rest,' Tobias told him.

'It's hotter than the Devil's armpit, and he's shivering under a blanket,' he muttered to me as we went back above decks. 'That can't be good, Anne.'

'He'll spring back,' I said stubbornly. 'Have some faith, Tobias.'

Tobias threw me an incredulous look, but he didn't try to have the last word, for once.

I wandered towards the bow, where a hot breeze fluttered the wings of my cap. I had my sketchbook in my pocket; I had thought to draw Horace whilst we talked. I was not really sure why I had wanted to do that, since he looked ghastly. I flipped through my sketches to the drawing I'd made of him in the stern that genial afternoon weeks ago.

'What do you see in him?' asked a voice.

I glanced up. Mr Tremaine was standing on the beakhead bulkhead, holding onto one of the foremast stays. He jumped down. 'Good afternoon, Miss Middleton. Truly, I'm curious. What do you see in our Horace?'

His dark eyes snapped in the late-afternoon sun, which floated on the horizon, waiting for the sea to douse its light. 'It isn't as though he's handsome. He's a pale, sickly, shrunken little specimen, if ever there was one. He'd best stay below in the next gale, or he will likely be tossed overboard.'

I was taken aback, and for a moment did not know how to reply. 'He is a pleasant person, Mr Tremaine. Mr Nelson is amiable, and intelligent, and gentlemanly. Besides, what have looks to do with anything? Some of the homeliest men I know have loving wives and devoted children.' I did not think Horace homely at all, but I didn't think that argument would serve me with Mr Tremaine. 'What makes you so caustic against him, anyway? Did you wish him to fail, this morning?'

Midshipman Tremaine's eyes narrowed almost imperceptibly, then they softened, anything resembling malice vanishing. 'I don't know,' he admitted. 'He *is* an agreeable fellow. Sometimes, though, I want to say things to him that are hurtful. I can't really say why he rubs me that way. Perhaps it is because he is so damned determined to be made lieutenant, and him not yet eighteen. He said the other day that he hoped to be the youngest man to take post in a generation. As though the rest of us have no ambition to ever be anything more than midshipmen.'

'I am sure he does not mean *that,* about the rest of you lacking ambition. He is singular in his aspirations, to be sure, but I do not think he means to disparage any of the rest of you.'

'Some days I think he might just do it, too,' Mr Tremaine mused. 'I did expect him to fall flat on his face, this morning… but I don't know if I actually wished it. I can't have done,' he said, more to himself than to me.

'I suppose it is only a competitive spirit, Mr Tremaine, and you do not actually wish him ill.' But even as I said this, something stirred uneasily in my breast.

*But the thing with the fork was only an accident. Even Horace believes that, and it was* his *arm that suffered.*

The ship's bell was struck eight times, in four sets of two clangs, signalling the changing of the watches.

'I must go,' Mr Tremaine said, 'I have this watch. I hope I may speak with you again, Miss Middleton.'

'Of course,' I said politely. I watched him walk away, telling myself that I had nothing to fear from Mr Tremaine. Nor from his little heathen statue.

I was wrong.

# PART III

I sat for a while with Horace the following morning. I was dismayed to find that he was so weak from fever that he could barely lift his head, and his stomach was sick, on top of it. But he begged me to stay, if only for a short time.

'I asked Bart if he'd ever had his dream again,' he murmured. 'And he said he had, the same night that our terrible dreams recurred.' He sipped carefully at a mixture of tepid water and ginger root juice. 'I don't know what it means, though.'

'Did you ask him if he died in his dream, this time?'

'I did. What he told me was more horrible than that. He said that they thought he had died, and they sealed him up in a coffin and buried him, whilst he was still alive.'

I felt a chill run over me from my head to my toes, and I shivered almost as badly as Horace had been shivering yesterday. 'That's horrifying.'

'I agree. I just cannot think how it is that we are all dreaming these evil dreams on the same nights.' His face went suddenly grey, and he closed his eyes and swallowed hard, several times. I dove underneath his cot for the basin, but he did not require it. 'I'm alright. It passed. Will you take this?' He held out the cup. 'It is better, for some reason, if I lie almost flat.'

I put his cup on the table and helped him lie flat, with only his head and the tops of his shoulders supported by the pillow. 'I have a theory,' he offered. 'But it defies logic.'

'This whole situation defies logic. Perhaps that is the only way to think about it.'

'Have you ever done anything to make Mr Tremaine… disinclined… towards you?'

'Mr Tremaine? Why, I've hardly spoken to the man. As a matter of fact, we have not had any conversation of consequence until yesterday evening.'

'What did you talk about yesterday evening?' Horace asked.

'Oh… things… it was not actually of much consequence, I guess. Just… pleasantries.' I was not prepared to imply that Mr Tremaine harboured any ill will towards Horace, not until… well, not yet, anyway.

'That might be enough to make him resentful, if you have not paid him much mind, yet you have spent quite a lot of time with me.' He dried his damp face with the bedsheet. 'I sometimes think that Mr Tremaine does not actually like me very much, for all that I originally thought him an agreeable person.'

'Perhaps it is merely that he harbours a competitive spirit, and he feels compelled to compete with you.'

'Thomas Troubridge and I competed with one another, but I never felt that Troubridge wanted to hurt me,' he said, almost inaudibly.

'Even if it is true, and Mr Tremaine *intended* to stab you with the fork, how could he be making us dream? And why is it affecting Tobias and Bart, too?'

'Mm. Tobias and Thomas Tremaine are of a similar age, and have similar personalities, have you noticed that?'

'It is rather hard not to.'

'I wonder if your brother threatens Mr Tremaine is some manner…'

'Tobias, threaten anyone? He might tease them to distraction…'

'Some people cannot abide being teased,' Horace murmured.

'Alright, let us say for the sake of argument that Tobias offended Mr Tremaine somehow. We still don't know how Bart fits into the equation. And how is he doing it? Has he put a curse on us?'

I was being whimsical, but Horace nodded tiredly. 'Not intentionally, perhaps. Do you think you can find out if there is anyone aboard who knows about *djinns?*'

'Djinns? What are those?'

'They are some sort of spirit in the Muslim religion, I think. Like Lucifer's angels, maybe. There are Muslims in India; I think they sometimes clash with the Hindus.'

'I'm afraid I am not following you, Horace. What can djinns have to do with Mr Tremaine?'

'Not with Mr Tremaine, at least not directly. With Mr Tremaine's ugly bronze figurine.' He seemed suddenly exhausted. 'When he showed it to me, he said it was supposed to… give a person power. And that it could grant wishes.' He could barely keep his eyes open.

'You think this horrid statue has something to do with djinns?' I asked uncertainly.

'I told you it was illogical…'

His voice trailed off. I thought he had fallen asleep, but then he whispered, '…I think it harbours one.'

'How are we going to quiz the crew about djinns without word getting back to Tremaine?' Tobias asked. We were sitting in the tiny cabin I shared with my mother, Tobias sitting in the single chair, and I on the berth, keeping our voices low. It was almost unbearably hot.

'I haven't the first idea. Extremely carefully. We do not know how dangerous this thing might be… but if it can control our dreams, I think the answer is "exceedingly".'

'What could it do to us? Drive us mad…?'

I wound my damp handkerchief through my fingers. 'It might drive you and me and Bart mad. I mean, could it conjure up a krait, or give Bart the French disease, or put your head in a noose? But I'm afraid it might try to put an end to Horace. It might convince him to drown himself.'

Tobias blew his breath out in a gust. 'That's a hideous supposition, Anne.'

'I hope I'm wrong,' I whispered. 'But say there *is* some sort of… evil spirit… attached to that statue? Do you honestly think that Mr Tremaine could control it?'

'Have you ever seen this statue that Horace told you about?'

'No. And I do not want to. Horace said it made him feel unwell.'

'It might not have taken much to make Horace feel unwell. I think he'd been on the tipping point for days.'

'Maybe, Tobias, but I do not want you to underestimate the gravity of this thing!' I tossed the crumpled handkerchief on the mattress. 'Do you remember your horrid drawings? What if you were seeing this… *djinn?*'

Tobias looked uncomfortable, and I said, 'You felt ill after that, didn't you? If I remember rightly, you went to bed for the rest of the day.'

'Yes, I did. I felt as though I'd been touched by something nasty, and it had gotten inside of me somehow. Alright, Anne, you don't need to convince me. But if that's true, we are up against something we can't possibly fight.'

'That's why we need to find out if anyone knows anything about djinns.' I rubbed my temples with my fingers, trying to stimulate my brain. 'I don't think it has free reign, at least, not yet. I think something has to release it, and can draw it back again at will. Otherwise, we'd have probably gone mad already, and I doubt we would be the only ones. But we have to figure this out before Mr Tremaine loses control of it.'

'I'll bring it up tonight in the wardroom. I'll throw the bait out there and see if anything—any*one*—bites.'

After supper, I got my needlework out of my trunk and took it into the wardroom. I had not given it much attention since we left Calcutta, but—tradition be damned— I didn't think any prospective beau would be likely to choose to marry me on the strength of my embroidered table linens.

The second lieutenant and the purser were playing backgammon, and the surgeon was reading—or was pretending to read; I think he was actually asleep. The marine commander was writing a letter. My father was closeted at the desk in his cabin with all kinds of tedious documents having to do with the American colonies, and my mother was taking an evening stroll above, seeking an evening breeze.

Tobias sauntered into the wardroom and plopped himself in a chair. 'Can anyone tell me what a djinn is?' he announced to the room in general.

'It is a Moorish fairy-tale,' said the marine.

'Not exactly a fairy-tale,' said the chaplain. I had not noticed him sitting outside his tiny cabin. 'Any more than angels or demons are fairy-tales.'

'Are they angels, then?' Tobias asked, turning his attention to the chaplain.

'If they are, they are fallen ones,' the chaplain said. 'But it is said that they were formed by Allah out of smokeless fire. Their powers are worldly ones, however, and their motives are suspect.'

'Have you heard of the "One Thousand and One Nights"?' the purser asked Tobias.

'The Arabian stories? I've heard of them, yes.'

'The one about the prince and his magic lamp…? Fellow finds a lamp that contains a spirit? *That's* a djinn.'

'I thought everything turned out all wine and Damascus roses in that story.'

'That time maybe,' said the purser. 'But you can't trust a spirit.'

'What else do they say about them?' Tobias persisted.

'In the folklore, they are always tied to some object, like a ring, or a lamp… it depends on who you talk to how much autonomy they're possessed of. They're supposed to do your bidding if you conjure one, but nobody ever suggested that they have to *like* it.'

'Dangerous business,' said the chaplain censorially, 'talking of conjuring spirits.'

'Less dangerous than actually conjuring them, Reverend,' said the lieutenant, and the men laughed.

'So… this fellow with the lamp, could he command the djinn to go back into the lamp when he didn't want it running around loose?'

'I don't know, son. I suppose it would depend on how beholden to the prince the djinn thought it was… and who knows how a djinn thinks?' The purser tossed the dice from the cup and moved a piece, and the lieutenant groaned.

'This is quite interesting,' Tobias said, and for a moment I was convinced he meant it. 'Say this prince didn't want the spirit around any more. Could he banish it? Tell it to go away?'

'Why would he want it to go away?' asked the marine.

'Maybe it isn't as benign as he thought. Maybe it's getting ideas about using its powers in ways the prince doesn't like. Maybe it has turned malignant, and he's frightened of it. Just speculating,' Tobias said to the chaplain.

'Moorish spirits are not my vocation,' said the chaplain. 'Our Lord could certainly have banished them; in which case, the power of God working through a man might banish them, as well. But that, as you said, is only speculation.'

'Better than that, cork the djinn up in his bottle or whatnot, and pitch him into the depths,' said the lieutenant, rattling the dice in the cup. 'Might not banish him forever, but he'd not find anyone to let him out again, down there in Davy Jones' locker.'

'What made you bring up djinns?' the purser asked Tobias.

'Just wondering if it was one of those sailing myths, maybe a Lascar one. Like mermaids, or those things that are part man, part dolphin, and are supposed to grant wishes if you catch one.'

'Don't muck about with things you don't understand,' the marine said, and went back to his letter.

'Good advice,' agreed Tobias. 'Thank you. Good evening, gentlemen.' He strolled casually out of the wardroom. A few minutes later, I quietly returned my embroidery to my trunk, and followed him out.

'Well, you heard it,' Tobias said, as we met at the stern rail. 'I don't know if it helps any.'

'I was hopeful that the chaplain would say you could say a prayer and perform some kind of ritual and be rid of it.'

'Couldn't be that easy. But if we could figure out how to steal its idol, we *could* take the lieutenant's suggestion and throw it overboard.'

'We would have to be certain that the spirit was well and truly bound to that object before we did it,' I said. A hot breeze ran its fingers down my back, and I shivered. 'Otherwise, we'll have only made things worse.'

Tobias stared morosely at the dark sea. 'If it gets free of the statue and can't be returned to it, we'll be sunk,' he said hollowly.

'That is what I'm afraid of,' I agreed.

In the morning, we recounted what we'd learnt to Horace.

He was up, and seated at the table in the sick berth, but he looked drained and fragile. The surgeon hadn't released him back to the midshipmen's berth, but given what we thought we were dealing with, I far preferred to have him here. It seemed safer somehow.

'Well, we know more than we did before,' he said. 'Do you know, I think we can actually tell when the spirit is abroad, and when has been recalled to the idol… we all seem to be able sense it.'

'Do you think Mr Tremaine has to physically touch the statue in order to summon the spirit, or do you think  he can communicate with it from a distance?' I asked. Horace was the only one of us who had seen the thing.

'I do not know,' he said. 'And I am not likely to find out soon. The surgeon and the mate want to keep me here through another paroxysm to observe me. I can hardly blame them,' he conceded, resigned. 'I have not given them much reason for confidence.' He looked down at his journal. 'They will let me go on deck to record the weather, and they say they will allow me to calculate our position at noon today, and they are reserving judgment about tomorrow.'

Tobias looked at me. 'Then it will have to be you or me, Sister.'

I caught myself swallowing apprehensively. 'Do you think we could convince him to show it to the two of us together? Obviously, I cannot go into the midshipmen's berth to look at it, and we have to get it out onto the open deck.'

'You should approach him about it, Anne,' Horace said. 'Appeal to his male vanity.'

In another mood, I might have wondered what Horace knew about male vanity; at the time, he didn't seem to possess any. 'He did ask if he might speak with me again, the other day, and I said yes… but that was before you told me your theory about the djinn. Tobias, you will have to rehearse me, otherwise I'm afraid I'll get nervous and give us away.'

'We will rehearse you; but do not worry, dear sister… you know I've always said you were destined for the stage.'

'Really…?' said Horace, taking Tobias all too seriously.

'He does, but only to get a rise from me. Papa would as soon see me parading my talents under the arcades at Covent Garden before he'd see me on the stage.'

'Oh. But you do have an excellent sense of expression and drama. You interpreted all the roles in the plays wonderfully well. It was a pleasure listening to you read.'

'If you do have to stay here for any length of time, it would be my pleasure to read to you again. But I hope you will not be here long.'

'Anne is to be the wife of a diplomat and direct dinners and receptions for visiting dignitaries, and be the friend and hostess of expatriate Britishers everywhere,' Tobias said, only half ironically. This really was the future my father hoped for me.

'I shall simply have to arrange a series of evenings of dramatic readings, where neglected government ministers and their wives may come and sit in a circle and read plays aloud,' I murmured. 'Perhaps we could even do fancy dress.'

'Oh – you must let me be Sir Toby Belch!' cried Tobias.

'I shall, if only for the pleasure of finally being allowed to call you "Toby".'

Horace looked bemused. 'Never mind, Horace,' I told him. 'It is a long-standing gibe between Tobias and me. There are many.'

'I think it sounds like a perfectly good idea,' said Horace. 'But for the sake of propriety, I would avoid anything by Kit Marlowe.'

By afternoon, with coaching from Tobias and Horace, I thought I was reasonably prepared to take on Mr Tremaine. But though I wandered around the ship, trying my best to appear aimless and carefree, no opportunity presented itself. We all went to bed that evening with a sense of frustration, but thankfully, we were not plagued that night by our dreams.

Tobias and I were amidships on the spar deck in the mid-afternoon, comparing notes. We had decided to divide and conquer, but so far had had no luck.

Our hushed conference was disturbed by raised voices near the fore mast.

'There's no call to speak to me that way, sir.'

'Damn you for a dog, Howells! When I tell you to do something, I expect to see it done!'

Thomas Tremaine, the object of our search, was confronting of one of the seamen, his face red with anger. The other man, not very much older than Midshipman Tremaine, was standing his ground.

'I was about to, sir. I reckoned I needed to finish what I was already doing, first.'

Mr Tremaine spluttered. 'You are not to "reckon," Howells! If I give you an order, I want to see you jump.

Your insolence and disrespect shall be marked against your name!'

Seaman Howells' chest swelled. 'Now see here, puppy—
'

Tremaine whipped a finger into the sailor's face. 'I'll have you tied to a grating and flogged for threatening me!'

Howells made a move as if to lunge at Tremaine, and two of the other seamen quickly interceded, taking Howells's arms, murmuring to him as they drew him away. The midshipman almost ran at them, but instead he threw his hat on the deck, glaring after the men and shaking with rage. Tobias and I slunk away towards the rear companionway.

'I have never seen him lose his head like that,' Tobias said. 'Do you think…?'

'That it has to do with that idol?' I finished for him. 'I really hope not. But there is no way be sure.'

''Fore God, I hope it isn't getting away from him, Anne. I thought we'd have more time.'

'I know. I think we had best steer clear of him for the rest of the afternoon, but we may not get to wait for an opportune moment… if either of us gets a chance to ask him to show it to us, we need to take it. And we must make certain that we're both there when he does.'

'I wish we could get Horace involved as well,' Tobias said pensively. 'He could read the atmosphere better than either one of us.'

'You saw him this morning, Tobias. He was hardly fit to be out of bed. I think it's imperative that we keep him apprised of what is happening, but he's not well enough to play an active part. Not even on his recovery day.'

'Well, I think we need to ask his opinion about what we just witnessed. So I hope he's up to it.'

Horace shivered through Tobias' entire recounting of the altercation on the spar deck, and I was tempted to offer to hold his feet again, but I thought better of it when I considered having to explain to Tobias.

'That's unlike Tremaine,' Horace said. 'He has always been assertive when he had to be, but I have never seen him openly confrontational.'

'So you think, as we do, that Tremaine is losing control?' Tobias appealed.

'I'm inclined to,' Horace said softly. 'But if you are asking me if I have any better ideas, I'm afraid not.' He drew his blanket closer around himself. 'I hope I am not being too obvious if I say be careful.'

We passed the galley as we left the sick berth; despite the equatorial heat, the galley still needed to be lit to boil the beef, oatmeal, and pease. I pitied the cook; here he was, broiling by the stove, whilst Horace, about twenty feet away, shivered with chills. I knew that the heat from the galley was supposed to warm the sick berth in cold or wet weather, but it did nothing to dispel ague, or warm Horace's cold feet.

I found the surgeon in his dispensary. 'My brother and I were visiting Mr Nelson a moment ago, and he seems to be suffering terribly today with the ague. Would it be possible to warm a piece of three-pound shot at the galley stove, and wrap it in a towel, for his feet?'

He put down his pen. 'It is possible, but Mr Nelson has never requested it.'

'He is not requesting it; I am.' I said firmly.

'Then I will tell Mithers to see to it, Miss Middleton.'

'Erm… Mithers…?'

'Bart, if you prefer.'

'Oh, I see. Thank you.'

I turned to leave, but paused when he said, 'Miss Middleton. Your compassion does you credit. But might I ask why you feel compelled to advocate for Mr Nelson…?'

'Who else does he have who will do it for him, sir? I am sensible that you treat everyone on this ship with the same thoroughness and care. But… well, sometimes, I hope, just knowing that someone cares enough to do one extra thing might make the difference between mere survival and recovery.'

He did not smile; perhaps he thought me naïve. But he nodded. 'I will see it gets done, miss.'

The following day we crossed the equator and entered the northern hemisphere. There were some high spirits and officer-condoned hijinks, but nothing like the hilarity we'd seen on the passage to India, when men who had never crossed the equator before endured a rigorous initiation. Everyone on this trip had already crossed over at least once.

Horace didn't observe the crossing. I'd looked in on him after breakfast and found him too ill even to converse. He lay in his cot, his hand limp in mine.

'I almost wish myself at the bottom of the sea,' he moaned. 'At least it would be cool in the depths.'

Bart sponged Horace's forehead and chest with a wet cloth, thoroughly dampening his shirt, to allow the evaporation to cool him. They had removed the rest of his clothing, and covered his wasted legs with a sheet.

Horace's face and limbs had begun to fill out again when the fever loosened its hold on him, but I was alarmed at how quickly those gains seemed to have vanished. I had seen beggars in the Calcutta streets who looked healthier than he did. The beggars, at least, were not the colour of dirty chalk.

'All you must do is endure today. Tomorrow will be better. Don't give up, Horace.'

He did not seem to have the energy to open his eyes. 'I shall try not to. But it is hard today, Anne.'

Tobias and I did not know what the fallout might have been from the confrontation between Mr Tremaine and the sailor, but Tremaine remained elusive. I saw him at noon, in conversation with the master's mate, and he looked sullen.

Towards evening, as a hellish red sun drowned itself in the sea, a mist crept across the surface of the waves, caressing the sides of the ship with tattered fingers.

The master looked uneasily out over the water. 'I don't like that. It's unnatural. Not supposed to see fogs at the equator.'

Tobias and I stood at the lee bulwark in the waist, watching the mist gather as the light failed. Neither of us spoke, but I think we both knew what the other was thinking. I jumped when someone spoke behind us.

'Heared you was askin' about djinns, sir.' The man was addressing Tobias.

'Y-yes. How did you know?'

The sailor shrugged. 'Lieutenant were talkin' to another as I were scrubbin' the boards. What you want t' know about 'em?'

'Do they exist?' I interjected.

He looked directly into my eyes. 'I'd say they do, miss. And I know what they say, about 'em doin' folks's biddin', and makin' 'em rich and all. But they're evil spirits sent from Hell, every one. I know the place where they keeps 'em, see. It's a rotten old fort near Delhi. There's an ancient mosque inside, where they keeps all the evil djinns locked up in a dungeon under the stairs. I been there, and I'd sooner 'ave the skin flayed off me back than go there agin.'

'If they're locked up, how do they get out?' Tobias asked.

'Some'un meddles. Invites it, to get it to serve 'im. Djinn'll promise a fool anythin' to get free from that dungeon. Once't it's free though, better look out.'

'*Who* locks them up?'

'Holy men, I reckon. Not the likes o' you and me, anyway.' He spat over the side. 'If you comes across one, don't have nothin' to do wi' it.'

The sailor disappeared below decks, as Tobias and I stared after him.

There was only breeze enough to stir the mist that evening, but the atmosphere was tense and strange, charged with some kind of uneasy current. During the first watch, the captain gave the order to put a reef in the sails for the night.

It was time to retire, but no one seemed to be confident of sleep in that close, claustrophobic air. Thus, there were plenty of witnesses to what occurred next.

Tobias and I had been to see Horace again, but found him in an exhausted sleep. Tobias had squeezed his hand, and I whispered good night into his ear, but he had not so much as twitched.

We were together on deck, both of us even more disquieted by our visit to the sick berth. 'He'll be better in the morning,' Tobias asserted, as much to himself as to me.

The mist had continued to rise until it shrouded the masts. It was hardly heavy enough to describe as fog, but the way it drifted around the ship made us feel isolated and somehow embattled.

We had barely registered the unearthly shriek, and the shouts from above, when the man landed on the deck with a sickening sound. He was immediately surrounded by men and officers, but I saw him long enough to identify him.

It was the young seaman named Howells.


Howells was carried to the sick berth, neither completely dead nor very much alive.

We didn't sleep at all that night. A wind sprang up, seemingly out of nowhere, at around midnight, blowing away the strange mist and stirring up white caps. Tobias moaned, and spent the rest of the night huddled on deck by the lee side of the waist. Since I knew I would be unable to sleep anyway, I sat with him and kept him company.

The wind calmed in turn towards dawn, as the darkness turned to grey. As the sun broke the horizon, Tobias and I returned to the sick berth.

Horace was propped up on pillows in his cot, with a mug of something milky-looking for his breakfast. The seaman Howells was shrouded beneath a sheet on the other side of the sick berth, asleep, or unconscious.

Horace turned anxious eyes on us. 'What can you tell me?' he asked in an undertone. 'I'm better today, but I can't get up,' he added. 'I cannot use my legs.'

'Why?' demanded Tobias. 'Are they paralysed?'

Horace shook his head. 'Too weak,' he said. 'Will you take this?' he asked me, holding up the mug. 'I cannot stomach any more of it.'

'We can't tell you much,' Tobias said quietly, as though Howells might be able to hear us. 'We heard him scream, and another topman shouted, but it happened so fast. They'd been sent up to reef the sails. I suppose he lost his grip. But there was no wind!'

'There was later. I felt it,' Horace replied. 'The captain must have anticipated it. I woke when they brought Howells in, and I was not able to sleep again, so I felt the wind come up. He was conscious for a while, talking to the surgeon.'

'Did you hear what he said?' I whispered.

'Most of it, I think. He was adamant that there was a figure on the yard in the fog, where no one could have been. And he claimed it shoved him.' Horace rubbed his eyes tiredly. 'His back is broken,' he said 'His legs *are* paralysed.'

We spent that day in a pervasive gloom. The entire ship was subdued; everyone went about his business in a self-contained, perfunctory manner. The enthusiastic chatter of the previous day was completely forgotten.

Seaman Howell's breathing grew laboured and shallow as the day progressed, and he died that evening. I sat with Horace as they stitched the sailor's body into his hammock. Neither of us spoke.

'I fear it will be me, next,' Horace murmured as Howell's body was carried away, to await being committed to the deep in the morning.

I looked at him, resting against his pillows, so fragile in the failing light, and I felt tears gather in my eyes. 'Do not say that.'

'We must be realistic, Anne. I'm not getting any better. Today was a good day, yet I was too weak to get out of bed.'

'I don't accept that,' I said, stubbornly. I blinked back the tears, but one escaped and trailed down my cheek. 'I refuse to accept that.'

He found my hand and pressed gently. 'Do not make it harder for yourself. I am not afraid to go, and I will not be unhappy. To rest… it will be good to rest…' His voice trailed off.

I do not know what possessed me. I certainly did not think about what I did next. I leaned over his cot, and kissed him full on the mouth.

He must have been momentarily surprised, but only for a moment. Then he enthusiastically kissed me back.

When we broke apart, neither of us seemed to have anything to say. I don't know what he was feeling, but I was both embarrassed and tingling at the same time, and I simply did not know how to express that.

'I should go,' I said, after we gazed mutely at one another for an interminable time. 'You must sleep tonight, since your sleep was broken last night. You'll need your strength tomorrow when the ague returns. I shall come and see you in the morning.'

There was a bemused smile on those sensitive lips. 'Sleep well, Anne.'

'Sleep well, Horace.'

I walked down the deserted gun deck towards the stern. It was shadowy, but not threatening tonight. My mind was replaying that kiss, and the more I thought about it, the more I decided that I liked it. But as I neared the companionway that would take me to the wardroom, I heard a whispering sound that made the small hairs at the nape of my neck rise.

I glanced over my shoulder, but there was nothing behind me but the length of the dark gun deck. There was a rhythm to the murmur, almost like an incantation.

'*…don't have nothin' to do wi' it.*' I heard the sailor's warning in my mind, but I was slipping off my shoes to creep cautiously towards the source of the sound. I was already in this over my head.

'…didn't want this… never wanted this. I never *wanted* this! How can I make it *stop*…? It wasn't supposed to happen… I didn't want it…'

I silently passed the companion ladder and stopped, peering into the darkness near the captain's cabin. It was hard to see him, but I sensed, rather than saw, a movement in the gloom.

Thomas Tremaine was slumped against a gun carriage, his knees drawn up against his chest and his head buried in his left arm. He pounded his calf with his right hand. 'This wasn't supposed to happen…' His whisper became a single sob. 'I didn't want him to *die!*'

I backed up, slipped my feet back into my shoes, and made certain my heels were audible on the boards of the deck as I approached. 'Mr Tremaine?'

He stopped whispering, but he didn't respond to me. I had not expected he would.

'Mr Tremaine... are you alright?' My voice wavered apprehensively, but there was nothing to be done about that. I hoped he would not notice.

He was silent for a moment more, then said quietly, 'Fine. I am fine, Miss Middleton.'

He could not see me from where he was sitting, and I was momentarily glad; glad too that I was unable to see him. 'Very well, then... if that is the case, good night, Mr Tremaine. I wish you a peaceful evening.'

He did not return my farewell, or if he did, I did not hear him.


' *"I am the resurrection and the life", saith the Lord...*'

The company stood on deck as the chaplain spoke the words of the burial service over the body of William Howells. I tried to ignore the implications what I had heard last night, in the dark of the gun deck.

Mr Tremaine stood with the other midshipmen, looking stoic. The only person missing was Horace.

I'd been to see him this morning, as I had promised. He was consumed by ague again, but he'd tried to be cheerful, for my sake, I supposed.

*'The Lord gave, and the Lord hath taken away; Blessed be the name of the Lord.'*

Before I'd left him, I'd asked, 'Do you want me to ask them to warm a piece of shot to put at your feet again?'

'Was that you, who suggested the warm shot?'

I nodded. 'Did it help at all?'

'I think it did, a little.'

'Then I shall request it again, on your behalf.'

'Bless you, Anne.'

*No, bless you, Horace,* I'd thought, as I walked away.

'*...we commend his body to the deep, ashes to ashes, dust to dust, in sure and certain hope of the resurrection to eternal life...*'

We watched as the board holding Seaman Howells's body was tilted and his shrouded remains slid into the sea. I fought back tears and tried not to think of Horace Nelson.

We had all experienced disturbed sleep the night before, but none of us seemed to be able to identify any particular reason for it. If I had dreamt, I did not remember it, and Tobias said the same.

I'd pulled Tobias aside last night when I got to the wardroom, and we'd closed ourselves in the cabin that Tobias and Papa shared whilst I recounted what I'd heard.

Tobias swore. 'It's all going to the Devil, isn't it, Anne? I mean, we knew it when Horace told us what Howells thought he saw on the yard, but Tremaine himself believes he had something to do with it.'

'I think we're running out of time, Tobias. I'm really afraid Horace might be next. I don't think Tremaine wants anything to happen to him, not any more than he wanted something to happen to Howells. But this *djinn,* or spirit, or whatever it is, isn't beholden to Tremaine anymore.'

'This is insane. *We're* insane.' Tobias shook his head. 'If there were any other, *rational,* explanation, I wouldn't give a second thought to supernatural beings or things that creep through your head at night.'

'Ugh. Don't say any more.'

'I don't think it was listening to Tremaine in the first place. I think it was more... sensing his inclinations, and... corrupting them. I think Tremaine is as much as a victim as

Howells was. The only crime that poor calf committed was buying that idol in an Indian marketplace.'

'That sailor told us not to get involved with it, but it's too late for that, isn't it?'

'Yes. I think it's definitely too late.'


I tried to intercept Mr Tremaine as the company dispersed, but he sidestepped me and clambered down the companion ladder. If he was embarrassed that I'd heard him the night before, it was going to be difficult to talk to him, and it might be up to Tobias. Then again, if the spirit sensed we were gunning for it, it might not let either one of us get close to Thomas Tremaine.


The horrible dreams returned that night, but they didn't end with the krait. It seemed that I was tangled up in Tobias', Horace's, and Bart's dreams, too. The krait bit me, and I suffocated slowly and agonizingly, but I did not die. Or perhaps I *was* dead, but I still functioned. I stumbled through a nightmare landscape to the foot of a scaffold, where Tobias dangled, his face and tongue purple and swollen, and his opaque eyes bulging. A fresh grave lay just beyond, and muffled screams and thumps issued from the mound of soil covering the grave.

I ran in terror, my lungs bursting for air, and found myself on the deck of the *Dolphin*. I whirled in panic, searching… there was Horace, with one foot on the gunwale, his hand grasping the shroud. Before I could reach him, he lifted his other foot, and stood balancing on the side of the ship, above the waves.

*HORACE!* I screamed, but no sound issued from my mouth, because I was dead. I staggered for the ship's side, and reached for him, wrapping my arms around his waist. Then a towering wave grabbed us, and flung us both into the sea.

Tangled together, we sank deeper, deeper... the last thing I saw was Horace in my arms, his soft eyes staring sightlessly into eternity.

Tobias stared at me, looking sick. We were in the sick berth, and I had just finished recounting my dream. 'Damn me; I don't like this. My dream had both of you in it, too,' Tobias said, 'and Bart as well.' He rubbed both his hands over his face. 'After I hanged, they cut me down and threw me in a coffin, but there was already a body in it. It was rotten and horrible, with no nose on its face and its eyes all mad, but it was still alive, and it must have been Bart. They nailed the lid down on us, but instead of burying us, they tipped us into the sea. The coffin lid came off when we settled on the bottom, and I got out and tried to swim for the surface. I was tangled in seaweed that held me back, and when I looked it wasn't seaweed at all, but the arms and fingers of drowned men. And two of the drowned people were you and Horace.'

Horace's voice was so soft that we strained to hear him. 'I know I dreamed,' he said, 'and I know that you both were in my dream. But we were all dead, all three of us.' His eyes were huge in his drawn face. 'I don't know where we were, though. It looked like a crumbling old fort, or palace, under the water, and there were drowned ships in the forecourt. Neptune was sitting on a chair made of spiny coral and sea urchins, and sea snakes were swimming around his ankles. He wasn't happy to see us.' This speech seemed to take all his strength to deliver. 'Or at least, he wasn't happy to see *me*, but he told me I could stay. *Forever.*'

The fever seemed to be eating him up from the inside. He squeezed my fingers with the hand that lay in mine, but the pressure was slight and brief. He looked as though he'd lost more weight in the past two days.

'We have to get our hands on that thing,' Tobias' voice was grim. 'Even if we have to break into the midshipmen's berth and steal it. Otherwise, we're all going to go mad.'

'Tremaine is avoiding us, Horace. We wondered if this spirit isn't controlling *him*, now.'

'Don't know.' Horace shut his eyes. 'I suppose it is entirely possible. I felt the influence of that thing when I held it. It felt as though it was draining me, somehow.' His voice had no more force than a sigh.

'You're worn out. We'll let you rest.' I leant over his cot and kissed his burning forehead. 'Tobias and I will figure it out. I do not want you to worry about it now.'

'Just… be very careful,' he whispered, drifting into sleep.

Thomas Tremaine did not look much better than Horace did, and I imagine neither did Tobias or I. We came across him at the stern rail, slinging macadamia shells into the sea, one after another. It appeared he had not slept in a while.

'Mr and Miss Middleton,' he acknowledged, but without much apparent pleasure.

'Hello, Mr Tremaine,' I said, with as much warmth as I could summon. Even as tired as I was, it was really not difficult to feel compassionate towards him. He looked miserable. 'It has been a terrible couple of days, has it not?'

He made a sound of agreement; not really a word, but it communicated effectively nevertheless.

'It shook me,' Tobias said. 'That fellow Howells, he was about my age.'

'Yes. Mine as well.' Tremaine flung his last nutshell.

'Horace said Howells was talking about a shadow-figure on the mast, when they took him to the sick berth. He must have been raving. He apparently said it *shoved* him.' I saw Tremaine flinch when I said this.

'It was most likely a trick of that uncanny mist,' he mumbled. 'There cannot have been anyone on the yard except the top men, and mist cannot shove a man. The officers have questioned the other men who were up there. None of them are sure of what they saw before Howells fell.'

'I imagine he was out of his mind with pain,' Tobias offered. 'Horace could not say for certain what it was Howells thought he saw.'

'How is Mr Nelson?' Tremaine asked, politely.

'Not very well,' I said softly. 'Some days are better than others; I'm sure you know. But overall he seems much weaker than he was before.' I tried to keep my voice neutral.

'You must give him my best wishes.'

'You could certainly do that yourself,' I suggested. 'He appreciates visitors.'

'I am not sure he would appreciate *me*,' Tremaine replied. 'I once stabbed him with a fork.'

'He told me about that. He also told me you were not aiming for him.'

'I thought Horace considered you his friend. He said you once showed him a very unusual Indian artefact you bought. He said it was intriguing,' Tobias said. 'I got the impression that you did not share it with just anyone.'

'I do not often share it at all. I just thought he might appreciate it. I don't think everyone would.'

'Why? Is it unattractive?' I asked.

'I suppose that depends upon what you consider attractive. It is not pleasing to the eye, but it has a kind of… magnetism.'

'Now *I* am intrigued,' Tobias announced. 'Is it very old, do you think, this mysterious thing? Would you be willing to show it to me and Anne?'

Tremaine hesitated. 'It doesn't…'

He did not finish what he had begun to say, but I somehow heard him speak it in my head. *'It doesn't like to be looked at.'*

'Please, Mr Tremaine, I'd like to see it, too.' I thought of Horace's story of holding the thing and my mind screamed *No—no I don't!*, but I kept my face neutral.

Tremaine seemed to waver. 'Alright,' he said finally. 'But I must go on duty shortly. Tomorrow, at the start of the second dog watch. I'll meet you on the larboard side of the waist, by the rail.'

Tobias and I met each others' eyes, but we did not dare react. 'Thank you,' Tobias said. 'We'll look forward to it.'


I went to see Horace alone that night. I don't remember what Tobias was doing… it is possible I hadn't asked him to come along.

Horace was propped up against his pillows, asleep. Bart must have bathed him and washed his hair, because it lay in turbulent waves around his face. He smelled sweet and clean, like castile soap.

He must have rubbed emollient into his lip, as well, because it glowed softly in the light from the lanthorn. That glow was irresistibly inviting.

One of his pale, slender hands lay draped across his chest, and I slipped it into my own as I kissed him.

His eyes came open as I drew back from his face. 'Anne,' he murmured.

'Hello, Horace.'

'If you were thinking about that myth of the woman who kissed a hideous creature and turned him into a god, I don't think it will work.'

'You cannot blame a girl for trying,' I said softly.

'Try again,' he suggested.

Oh, it was lovely, kissing him. He was not aggressive in the least, but he returned the kiss with enough enthusiasm to let me know he liked it. I would have been happy to let it go on and on, but the thought of Tobias, our 'chaperone', popped into my head. Followed by Tremaine and the idol.

'How are you feeling?' I asked, when we were both in our proper places, a respectable distance apart, again.

'Drained. But the fever day is over, thank God. Tomorrow should be better. I'm hoping to get my appetite back. I could not keep anything down today.'

'I hope you do. You need to eat; you are far too thin again.' I caressed his knuckles, which stood out like knobby stones under the skin of his hand. 'Speaking of tomorrow… Horace, Tremaine agreed to show us the statue tomorrow afternoon. We're to meet him in the waist at the beginning of the second dog.'

He closed his eyes. *'Stand by to come about,'* he murmured. 'By God, Anne. I hope this works.'

'It must. Before someone else gets hurt.'

He turned his hand in mine and squeezed it firmly. 'I know,' he affirmed softly. 'I know.'


I'd expected the horrifying dreams to return that night, but I fell asleep thinking about that kiss I'd shared with Horace, and I don't believe I dreamt at all.

The day dragged, however. Tobias and I were tortured by the agonising slowness with which the minutes passed.

We'd visited Horace again after breakfast, and found him up, seated in a chair. It looked as though he'd made an effort to dress, even donning his waistcoat and stockings, but it must have taken a lot out of him, because his bearing was not at all animated. 'I'm alright for short periods,' he said. 'I can get around the sick berth, but I don't think I could walk the length of the ship yet.'

'There's no reason for you to walk the length of the ship, is there?' Tobias asked disapprovingly.

Horace shook his head. 'None but my desire to be useful again.'

'Do not rush your recovery,' I entreated him. 'You have had a bad couple of days. Don't try to do too much too soon.'

'My fear is that I will not be of any help to you in… in what you have to undertake today.'

'There are two of us, and… two… of them,' Tobias said slowly. 'And only one of *them* has a corporeal body. As long as Tremaine can keep the thing contained within its statue, this ought to be easy.'

'That's a rather large and uncertain condition,' Horace observed soberly.

My brother grinned with characteristic confidence. 'This thing might be thousands of years old, but it has never come up against a Middleton,' he said. 'It will never know what hit it.'


Thomas Tremaine was waiting for us when we approached the waist that evening. The sun was low, painting everything with a molten, golden light.

Tremaine held his arm close across his middle, as if he had a stomach-ache. He was actually holding the statue, wrapped in its handkerchief, under his coat.

'I got it from an old fakir for a handful of rupees and a bottle of rum,' he explained. 'I didn't think fakirs drank rum, but it was a bargain.' He carefully unwrapped the statue. 'He told me it came a place called Feroz Shah Kotla. As if that made it more authentic, somehow.'

The figure lay on its bed of wrappings. It was not large, only about five inches in length, and it *was* ugly. It had bulging topaz eyes and a tongue that dangled from its mouth. Its arms and one leg were lifted in some sort of grotesque dance, and its head was haloed with bronze flames.

'The fakir said it was powerful and could grant wishes. He told me to be careful what I wished for. But I do not believe in it.'

I looked up sharply and saw his eyes as he said this, and I could see that he lied. He might not have believed initially, but he did now. 'It's why I do not show it to most people. I do not want them to be encouraged to wish on it. But I was certain that our Horace would not be tempted.'

'Why is that?' Tobias asked.

'He's the son of a clergyman. He has God in his *veins*.' Tremaine picked up the statue and offered it to Tobias. 'But the statue is just a statue. Here, see for yourself.'

Tobias took the ugly little idol and turned it over in his hands. His face had been impassive, but I saw it change as he examined the artefact. He frowned, and his eyes acquired a bemused, then alarmed look.

'Anne.' His voice sounded strained. 'Take it…' He held out the statue. He was beginning to look panicked. 'I can't breathe.'

I grabbed the statue before he could drop it. He started choking, and Thomas Tremaine caught him and lowered him to the deck, loosening Tobias' stock and tearing at his throat button.

*I need to do it now,* I thought. *While Mr Tremaine isn't looking.* But I could not make my arm obey.

The statue writhed like a snake in my hands, and I tried to drop it, but I could not. The idol/snake struck, piercing my forearm, and I felt something – I can only describe it as energy – go out of the ugly piece of bronze.

I was still trying to fling the statue overboard, but as I raised my arm, someone wrested the thing from my grasp.

'*GO BACK! GO BACK!!*' Horace held the statue above his head, his back to the rail. '*GO BACK!!*' he shouted again.

I was paralysed. I did not know what he meant, or to whom his demand was directed. Tobias was gasping on the deck, his face gone an ugly shade, and my right arm was suddenly useless. But Tremaine was moving. He had left Tobias, and was launching himself at Horace.

*If Tremaine hits him, Horace will go over the rail with that statue.* Before I had even registered this thought, I was moving, too. Tremaine and I hit Horace at the same time: Tremaine dead-on, and I from the side.

We hit him so hard. His fragile frame went flying—sideways. He hit the boards with a sickening thud, and I saw his head strike one of the posts supporting the gunwale. The idol was still clutched in his right hand, which had ended up underneath the rail, dangling over the ship's side.

'Yes…' he breathed. And he let go.

I watched the statue glance off the tumblehome and drop into the sea. And Mr Tremaine went after it.

*'MAN OVERBOARD!!'* Tobias cried. He was back on his feet. *'MAN OVERBOARD!'*

The numbness in my right arm was gone, and I scrambled to Horace on my hands and knees.

'Horace? *Horace!'* I knelt beside him, cradling his head in my hands. I could not see any blood, but neither could I tell whether he was alive. 'Oh merciful God, please…please.'

I had lost my cap, and my hair had come loose from its pins. I could feel the wind blowing it about my head, and I sensed warmth from the setting sun on my back. That golden light washed over Horace as he lay, ominously still, on the deck.

Around us, noise and activity whirled like a cyclone as the crew got a boat in the water, but I was only peripherally aware of any of this. My only concern was for Horace.

Horace's eyelids fluttered; he blinked slowly. His eyes closed once more, then opened again. They were unfocused, and I did not know if he was seeing me at all.

'Horace…?'

'Nelson will be a hero…' he murmured.

'Mr Nelson, you already are,' I told him, as Bart, who had been summoned to the deck with the surgeon's mate, lifted him to carry him below.

Horatio was exceedingly bruised, and he had an awfully large lump on his head where it had struck the post, but it seemed to have knocked the fever out of him. The surgeon kept him in the sick berth for another week, but his recovery was rapid from that point. Though he was not yet as strong as his fellow midshipmen, he was no longer an invalid.

I had two ugly punctures on the inside of my forearm, most likely from the points of the bronze flames that had surrounded the little idol's head. They healed fairly quickly, but I can still find the scar if I look.

Tobias suffered no physical injuries from the ordeal, but his manner became more measured and mature. He no longer teased me quite so much. I missed it, a bit.

Thomas Tremaine was retrieved from the sea with only a bit of it in his lungs. He and Horatio repaired their relationship over the two days that Tremaine was held in the sick berth for observation. Horatio later told me privately that he thought Tremaine was recovering from something more than just a dunking in the ocean.

'Who were you talking to, on the deck, when you cried "go back"?' I asked him.

He looked out over the water, not answering immediately. Finally, as though speaking to the sea, he said, 'The djinn. I was commanding it to go back into the statue.'

He turned his head to look at me. 'I'd felt it leave the idol when you were holding it, and I knew it was loose. If it did not go back into the statue, I couldn't let you throw the thing into the sea.'

I shuddered. If Horatio had not been there, I *would* have thrown the figure into the sea, and the djinn would have been free.

If it actually was a djinn. The farther we got from the events, the less real they seemed.

Horatio had stopped being 'Horace' after the statue went into the sea. It seems Horatio is a hero's name.

He, Tobias, and I continued to see one another for a time in London, and he and I shared a final kiss before Horatio, a newly minted lieutenant, joined his new ship bound for the Channel.

I had often hoped I might see him again, but his service to King and Country always came first. I sometimes tell myself that had his road not been so long and hard, he might have come back…

But my gain might have been our country's loss, and he was always destined to be a hero.